IN THE TIME OF THE RUSSIAS

by

Stella Zamvil

John Daniel, Publisher

SANTA BARBARA

1985

ACKNOWLEDGMENTS

"On Going to Jerusalem" and "Petrashka" were first published in *The Reed*. "Lyuba" was first published in *Descant*. "The Wedding" was first published in *Young Judaean*. "Summer's Idyll" was first published in *Northwoods Journal*. "The Match" was first published in *Jewish Dialog*. "Out of Egypt" was first published in *Centripetal*. "Nissun's Dawn" was first published in *Rhino*. "In The Time of the Russias" was first published in *Quarter-Two, Another View*. "Schmiel Pinhas" was first published in *Gusto*. "Lemish's Wife" was first published in *Waves*. "Dybbuk in the Soup" was first published in *Palo Alto Review*. "The Doctor" was first published in *Foreground*. "And Next Year" was first published in *Mamashee*.

Cover photograph courtesy of
The Library of Congress
Design by Jim Cook
Typography by Cook/Sundstrom Associates
SANTA BARBARA

LIBRARY OF CONGRESS CATALOGING IN PUBLICATION DATA
Zamvil, Stella, 1926-
In the time of the Russias.
1. Jews—Soviet Union—Fiction.
2. Soviet Union—History—19th century—Fiction. I. Title.
PS3576.A48I5 1985   813'.54   85-4485
ISBN 0-936784-02-4 (pbk.)

Published by
John Daniel, Publisher
P.O. Box 21922
Santa Barbara, Ca. 93121

IN THE TIME OF THE RUSSIAS

On Going to Jerusalem

FETTER SHEEYAH woke one morning with one thought in his head: today he would leave for Jerusalem. He notified his son of his intention as soon as he unwound his tefillin and tucked them back into their little velvet bag after chanting his morning prayers. Chaim greeted his father's declaration with an indulgent smile as he continued to eat; after all Papa was eighty-four, and Jerusalem at least thirteen thousand miles from Lvov. So Chaim smiled and said,

"Sure Papa, after breakfast."

Fetter Sheeyah began to take his few belongings and fold them into a small "packel" made of the ticking of an old pillow to be carried over his shoulder.

"Ruth," Chaim called quietly as his wife was clearing the table and when she glanced at him he nodded his chin in Fetter Sheeyah's direction. In that corner of their large one-room cottage Fetter Sheeyah was methodically putting his belongings into his pillow-slip pack—his tallis and siddur carefully placed on top. Then he walked into the kitchen area and took some bread out of the cupboard, some cheese from the drawer, wrapped them in cloth and tucked them into his pack which he held by its neck in one hand.

9

Ruth and Chaim exchanged glances. Fetter Sheeyah was serious. He was most exact in this preparation of his personal items.

"Father, this is ridiculous—you've made no plans for a trip. This takes time. Sit down. Let's talk it over."

Fetter Sheeyah glanced at his son, smiled with raised eyebrows and continued his search for sundry objects in the house. After a while he sat down on his bed in one corner of the room and inspected the soles of the shoes he was wearing, went to the closet and took out his other almost-discarded worn ones and put them into his pack.

Ruth and Chaim watched helplessly. They tried to engage him in an argument, but Fetter Sheeyah waved them off.

"Father, be reasonable. You can't leave now just like this!"

Chaim turned to Ruth as the proceedings were reaching frustrating conclusion.

"Can one become Oyva Buttal overnight?"

"Oh, no, Chaim. I can't believe that your father has suddenly become senile."

Fetter Sheeyah was checking his old coat before it was to go into the sack on his back. Chaim spoke to Ruth without taking his eyes off his father, "Go see if Dr. Oblensky is in—find him and bring him here immediately."

She flew out the door without even taking her shawl.

Chaim braced himself near the doorway wondering if he were going to have to use force to keep his father from leaving.

Fetter Sheeyah faced him, sack in hand.

"Why should you want to keep me from going?"

"Why? Father, are you out of your mind to talk about such a trip?"

"Out of my mind? To do now what I have wanted to do all my life? I have even waited longer already to make my journey than our great poet Yehuda Halevi did."

"But it's impossible to just walk out of a house on the spur of the moment—it's crazy!"

"Crazy? No, I would be crazy if I didn't do this now. I may have already waited too long."

He tried to walk by Chaim.

"Father, please be reasonable." Chaim held his arms toward his father. The doctor, followed by Ruth at his elbow, brushed by Chaim's outstretched hands.

"Fetter Sheeyah," Doctor Oblensky breathed huskily, "How are you feeling today?"

"Fine, Dr. Oblensky, thank you. Why shouldn't I be?"

"Ruth tells me you're planning a journey—to the Holy Land?"

"Yes, that's true. It has long been planned. I'm only putting it into effect."

"Couldn't you delay it only a little while?"

"For what good reason? Time doesn't always work for us, especially at my age. Tell me, have you a good reason to keep me? I have done all that was needed and expected of me here. My sons are good, grown men—responsible, religious, kind men. Since my wife, your mother, died," he addressed himself to Chaim, "I have been marking time. Soon I will be called upon to meet the Almighty. Where and when this happens will be His choice, not mine or yours." He looked at Dr. Oblensky. "I am not concerned with the hazards of my journey, because I am not greedy any longer—I have been blessed with many years on this earth already. I am not seeking danger. If the Almighty decrees that I meet Him before I reach Jerusalem, it will be so whether I go or stay. It is only in His hands—His decree will hold, and His wishes."

"You haven't seen any visions, have you, Fetter Sheeyah? Or heard any voices?" asked Dr. Oblensky.

"No. I am not deranged. My thoughts are rational. My mind is not wandering. This desire I express is not new, it's one dear to the hearts of all Jews. Why should you even wish to deny it to me? Only He can decide my worthiness." He looked at them with clear earnest eyes. They had no answer. Shrugged. Looked at each other.

"Couldn't you wait another day or two, Papa, just so we can put the right things together for you? And we could write ahead to Eva in Odessa? I'm sure that is the route you will wish to follow. We could check out the roads and plan your stops in the..."

"Don't worry. I know my directions and which roads to follow."

"The Cossacks have been moving artillery toward the Austrian border. There is talk of a pogrom in Kiev. Wait a bit, Fetter Sheeyah," said the doctor.

Fetter Sheeyah moved past them across the threshold, kissed the mezzuzah on the doorpost.

"Hashonah ha ba bi Yerushalayim." (And next year in Jerusalem.)

"Doctor, tell me what to do. Shall I hold him by force—my own father? Tell me is he sick or senile?"

Dr. Oblensky shook his head.

"He seems as rational as you and I, and yet what he plans to do is sheer insanity. One doesn't walk from the Russian Ukraine to Jerusalem!"

"I'll walk with you a way, Papa," Chaim said to his father as he walked away from the house. "Ruth, please get me my jacket."

Ruth ran for it, but they were well past the well when she reached them, panting. The doctor was still in the doorway watching the two men, Fetter Sheeyah dressed as he might be for the synagogue, in his best clothes and hat, taking short sprinting steps. Chaim walked with longer thoughtful steps beside him until noon.

Then with the sun high, Fetter Sheeyah sat down under a tree and opened his pack. He took out a piece of bread, said the prayer before eating, and broke off a small piece of bread, took a few bites and offered a piece to Chaim who waved his hand negatively at it. So Fetter Sheeyah took a few more small bites, and brushed the crumbs from his shirt. He watched his son's eyes upon him—the day was going and Chaim was thinking of his wife. He owed his family his allegiance, but this was his father.

"Go home, Chaim. You have walked me far enough. I will be all right, you'll see. I will write as soon as I arrive. Eva will write for me from Odessa. Go—your responsibility to me has been more than fulfilled. You have been a good son to me—and Ruth a sweet, loving daughter."

He picked up his pack, anchored his broad brimmed hat more securely on his head, brushed and neatly tucked his beard as he surveyed the road ahead. He turned quickly to Chaim, shook his hand quickly and turned his face toward the road. Chaim stood watching him until he disappeared, the road curved, hidden by a large clump of trees which stood at the edge of the forest.

Fetter Sheeyah's trousers collected the dust of the road; little twigs and dried leaves caught in the wool of their cuffs. He sat down occasionally and nibbled on his bread and cheese, and sampled the water of young springs breaking through the ground.

Toward sunset he stopped to say his evening prayers and prepare for the night. He slept soundly until he was awakened by shouts and clanking wheels. Children ran by the road close to him. He got up, straightened his clothes, and picked up his pack which he had rested his head on through the still warm autumn night. A man yelled at him and began to walk toward him. A big, husky farmer. He looked at Fetter Sheeyah, in his careful though somewhat crumpled attire—his hat, his pack—his beard.

"What are you doing here?" he asked Fetter Sheeyah.

"What am I doing here? Nothing. I slept here and now I can continue on my way."

"Where are you from?"

"Lvov."

"Go home, old man."

"I can't. I must continue."

"This is a dangerous way for you to come. The peasants are not happy with Jews, and they would need little excuse to kill you."

"If I am to die, I will die," said Fetter Sheeyah, swinging his pack on his back.

"What town are you going to, old daddy? There may be some back roads for you to take—safer ways."

"I'm going to Jerusalem."

"To Jerusalem? From Russia?"

"Yes, Jerusalem, the Holy City."

"By foot?"

"By foot." And then to explain further, "Of course, by boat most of the way from Odessa."

Peasants running by stopped and closed in about them.

"Kurka—a Jew!"

"Let him have it!"

"Wait," said the farmer. "He's only a crazy old man—he's going to Jerusalem. Let him go."

"Let him carry some of our sins with him!"

One of the peasants thrust a pitchfork at his back. The farmer deflected the blow without knocking the pitchfork from the peasant's hand.

"Save it for a while. The Cossacks will give you something to jab at. I hear they're fighting on the Austrian border. The guns will be shelling us soon. Let the old Jew go. The Cossacks or the guns will finish him off."

Fetter Sheeyah let no time elapse in putting space between himself and the group of peasants. The morning prayers and the washing and breakfast would have to wait. Before long he came to a clearing of soft grass bounded by low hedges flecked with an occasional blackberry bush. Here he stopped. But there was no water. There were no houses in sight. No springs or wells. Washing would have to wait.

The shrinking bread was brought out. A bit of cheese, very dry but adequate. The grasshoppers sang and jumped in the grass about him. The bees lazed in the sun-warmed air.

A rumble was suddenly heard and the birds left the few trees they were in. Dull thuds became heavier and louder. Two troops of mounted Cossacks appeared from opposite directions. The two leaders converging drew their horses along side each other, considered their respective orders, counseled briefly together and galloped on, their troops streaming after them.

Fetter Sheeyah watched from the shade of young twin elms under which he had moved his pack. He waited for the slow moving line to pass and leave the road clear. The line was endless. Slow, pulsing, rumbling. Horsemen galloped by periodically. Suddenly the line halted.

Guns were dismounted and fixed in the ground. The cannons faced him. A new battleline was being formed. He picked up his pack and began to walk toward the lines of cannons quickly. A Cossack lieutenant on horse saw him approach and galloped toward him, saber in hand. Fetter Sheeyah gripped his pack tightly with one hand, held up his free hand, waved and yelled at the Cossack officer.

"I am not the enemy. I come from Lvov."

The Cossack swung his saber toward Fetter Sheeyah when suddenly the ground buckled and his horse shied. The saber missed Fetter Sheeyah as he stood still, one hand raised. The Cossack rode back to muster the men at the lines. The peasants were dropping their equipment and flying into the wagons. The Cossacks tore after them.

Fetter Sheeyah walked toward the firing lines. A few bewildered men stood there wiping their perspiration, clearing the mountings of the few manned cannons.

"You were very lucky, old father," said one young soldier. "I saw one such Jew as you eating his own beard yesterday in Pinsk."

Fetter Sheeyah walked on. When things quieted he would cross the Austrian border. He would head south to the waterways. A little saved money at the bottom of the pack would buy his passage. In Constantinople he could stay with a religious sect of Jews for a few days, observe the holidays and continue on his way. If he were lucky and the winter not too severe, he would make Jerusalem before next year. Even when the possibility of dying enroute occasionally clamored, he brushed it aside. God's will be done.

God's will would be done. For three weeks he walked, making his way from village to village. Finding the synagogue if the number of Jews in the town warranted one, or the occasional lone Jew who would guarantee him a meal and often a night's lodging with whatever comfort and warmth the family could share, and with that their troubles and fears. Hard tales were being relayed— and where could one run?

The borders were closed and guarded. The only ones left unwatched were those under shellfire from both sides, or constantly changing in battle as one side advanced and the other retreated like waves washing over the shore. One moment the sand belonged to the sun, and the next to the water. The villages caught in such a barrage of fire never knew whose shells were falling on them—their own or the enemy's.

When he reached Odessa, Eva tried to keep her uncle with her. She fed him, cleaned his clothes, and finally in despairing defeat, had both pairs of his shoes resoled. Fetter Sheeyah wanted to be in Constantinople for Passover.

"Fetter Sheeyah," Eva told him as she folded his clothes back into his pack, "you are an oxshin. No one is so stubborn, so single-minded as you. Look at all the room I have here. Yonkel is married and living with his wife's family. I'm so lonely I'll have to let rooms out just for company—not that I can't use the few groshen the rooms will bring in. It's a nice house, old, but large and with the children grown it's a very empty house. Do stay."

She put her hand on his arm and poured him another cup of tea. But Fetter Sheeyah wanted to be in Constantinople for Passover.

Eva went with him to the wharf and listened for news of a boat going to Constantinople. The war kept the boats from leaving with their customary frequency, but finally an arrangement was made with the captain of a ship delivering coal. Constantinople was one of the ports where he would discharge part of his cargo and pick up spices.

Fetter Sheeyah discovered on board ship that he could keep more settled by not watching the bounce of the horizon as he focused his eyes on the far distance. He would wait below for the captain to tell him when land was in sight, or driven up by the stuffy confines of the room he shared with three other travelers, he would anchor his eyes to the blue sky to cushion the roll and toss of the ship as it moved under his feet.

Fetter Sheeyah observed Passover in Constantinople, staying with a group of scholarly Chasidim, and then booked passage on a ship carrying lumber to the Holy Land. This journey was brief and the Mediterranean kinder than the Black Sea had been. They landed in Jaffa and from there Fetter Sheeyah continued on to Jerusalem. A few more days' walk, an occasional borrowed donkey ride and he made his entrance into Jerusalem on a cold windy day.

Unlike the great twelfth century poet, Yehuda Halevi, who was killed by an Arab horseman as he knelt to pray his thanks at beholding the gates of the beloved city, the city of his dreams and poems—Jerusalem, Fetter Sheeyah enjoyed a few short years in the Holy Land. But the letter he sent his children to tell of his joy had no one to read it. All the Jews—men, women, and children—of the village had been slaughtered in the pogrom triggered by the defeat of the Cossacks in their first battle of the war with the Austrians.

Lyuba

THE SKY was blue, crystalline blue with white morning clouds puffed by wind moving gently, slowly. A woman, small and heavy-set, wearing thick peasant clothes, walked across the bare ground toward the barn. Carefully looking behind her, she opened the door of the barn and called in distinct but hushed tones,

"Lyuba! Lyuba!" She looked inside. She could hear the straw moving in the darkness. "Lyuba? Are you there?"

"Mamushka?" A strained voice answered. "Yes, I'm still here."

"Lyuba, quick. Get ready to go."

The blonde head of her daughter appeared and peeked out the door. Tall and slim, the young woman moved into the sunlight shaking straw from her blonde plaits and cotton dress.

"Mamushka, the horse. Is Linka saddled?"

"Yes! Yes! She is on the far side of the meadow . . . waiting." She undid the kerchief from her head with trembling fingers and thrust it on the girl. "You'll need this, too." She took a small bag from her apron pocket and put it into her daughter's hand. The girl tried to refuse, but her mother brushed her off, walking by her rapidly behind the barn toward the meadow. They climbed silently over the hillock.

"Does Papa know?" Lyuba asked. "He doesn't suspect?"

18

Her mother shook her head.

"Fanya?"

"Fanya! Don't ask!" She stopped momentarily puffing in the cold air. She waved her hand frantically as she fought to catch her breath. "Let's not talk about Fanya! Quick, Lyuba. . . ." She grabbed her daughter's arm and moved her up the hillock. "The Cossacks have been around, they're asking questions."

"If Misha comes, tell him I'll be in. . . ."

The mother quickly reached for her daughter's mouth and stopped her voice with her fingers.

"Don't tell me, Lyuba! I don't want to know." They came toward the horse standing in the meadow below the hillock. "I don't know why you have to do this—why you?"

Lyuba turned to her when she reached the horse. "How many times have I told you, that it is for us who see what is wrong and know what can be done, it is for us to do it. Not to hide ourselves or pray for it."

"This is what comes from sending to the university. . . ." The mother spat at the earth. "Better to live. . . ."

"How, Mama? Like a vegetable? Like Papa?" She mounted the patient chestnut. Sarah moved close to the horse and checked the cinch. "Do you think he will pray us all into heaven?" Lyuba asked smiling.

The mother moved back and looked at her daughter. "Sometimes I think you do not give your father credit. . . ."

"Come, Mamushka," Lyuba reached down from the horse, "a kiss." Sarah reached her arms around the girl and hugged her, then pushed her off. "Go, child, go. . . if you must do this," she finished to herself. The horse and the blonde flowing head disappeared around the next ridge.

She glanced toward the house. Tatushka might become suspicious. She was out so long. Walking quickly past the barn she picked up the empty pail standing near the barn door and decided to get a few more drops from Manya, the cow. It was well into the morning and Manya might not mind too much.

"Yechiel. Tatushka!" Sarah called as she entered their small house and set the pail on the earthen floor.

"Sarah! Here!"

She looked in the direction of the voice and saw him sitting on the bed in the farthest side of the room, reading a book. Always reading. Studying. Trying to pry meaning from the texts, as if the reason for his existence could be found in their words. The books. The same books his father had read before him and his father's father, and his father before him. The edges of the pages flaked, but the ink held dark and clear, as he examined them over and over. Sometimes she wondered in his intensity, if this was in the service of God or self. The way of scholars, she shrugged.

She lifted the lid from the large pot and stirred the soup with a large ladle lying on the stove, when suddenly she was aware that Yechiel was standing and watching her.

"You were outside a long time," he said.

"I went to get a little more milk."

"Milk? We can't use it for supper."

"True. We're having a meat soup tonight, but I had cramps during the night, and a little hot milk usually helps." She turned back to the cooking for a moment. He stood for a while looking at her, scratched his neck under his beard and returned to his books.

Sarah then tidied up the kitchen. Toward noon she heard someone walking up to the house. Who? She expected no one and cocked her head expectantly. A knock.

"Enter!" she called toward the door as she stepped to it.

"Mamushka."

"Fanya! Come in!" She recognized the voice. "The door is unlocked...." She pulled it open. There stood a tall dark beautiful woman, elegantly dressed in a dark blue wool suit with large matching hat, holding a small child by the hand.

"Here, go to your grandmother." The woman moved the little boy toward Sarah.

"Come, little one." Sarah gathered the little boy into her arms.

"Yechiel, come see who is here!" she called to her husband.

He got up from the bed and walked to them. He smiled at little Benjamin and patted his blonde head, pinching his cheek before returning to his reading. The two women sat down on the stools Sarah had moved closer to the stove.

"Take off your jacket. It will be too cold when you go out again." Sarah rubbed the little boy's hands to warm them and sat him on her lap. Fanya removed her hat and set it on her lap, then slowly unbuttoned her jacket. When the kettle began to steam, Fanya fixed tea for her mother and herself. They spoke softly not to disturb the old man.

"Your husband is well?" Sarah asked, as they sat near each other.

"Vassily is well, thank you," Fanya answered.

Sarah held the glass of tea Fanya had poured for her out of the child's reach. She sipped it slowly and set it next to Fanya's on the cooled metal of the stove. Her daughter looked well, she noticed, but a little worried. Twice Fanya began to say something, but the words fell away from her lips unsaid.

"More tea, Mamushka?" she asked holding the hot kettle.

"No, dear, thank you. We'll be eating soon. Won't you and Benjamin eat with us, please?"

Fanya shook her head. Her dark hair cascaded over her shoulders. "No, Mama. Vassily will be home soon."

"He isn't with his unit in the north?"

"No. He is stationed near town this week."

"Near town?" The child began to fret and his mother reached her arms out to him, but Sarah waved her off and began to bounce him on her knee.

"They're afraid of trouble here," Fanya said slowly, in very soft deliberate tones as she looked hard at her mother.

"Trouble?" Sarah looked into her daughter's eyes unflinchingly.

"They are afraid that we have traitors among us—Revolutionaries."

Sarah handed Benjamin to Fanya, stood up and turned her attention to the soup simmering on the stove. She uncovered the pot and stirred the soup.

"We can't afford that, Mama."

"What?" asked Sarah.

"We can't harbor traitors."

"Who is a traitor, Fanya?"

"Mama! Anyone who opposes the Czar. You know that."

"The Czar takes care of our people, huh, daughter, with his Black Hundreds—pogroms?"

Fanya stood up angrily.

"Mama! I am trying to protect you and Papa!" She quieted as she remembered and glanced toward her father. Oblivious to their conversation, Yechiel was sitting on his small wooden bench, his tallis over his shoulders, saying the evening prayers, peacefully absorbed he read, reciting the words with his lips.

"Small thanks! We have traitors among our own. . . ." Sarah hissed, her eyes following Fanya's glance set on Yechiel. He had cut wood for her yesterday, too much too long, and his cough had returned. He could not move from the bed that night. Sarah felt her hand grabbed by Fanya.

"What I do also protects you, remember that!" she dropped her mother's hand and seizing the child began to walk out of the house. As she reached the door, Fanya turned back to her mother.

"Linka is not in barn."

Sarah was spooning soup into two bowls, and without looking at her daughter, she answered, "Papa lent her to the Stramskys for the day."

"Remember, Mama, what I do is to protect you, Papa—our people—I have to—whatever I do," she cried hoarsely and ran out, hat in one hand, dragging Benjamin with the other.

"I don't thank you!" Sarah shouted after her daughter through the open doorway, and knit her brows as she pondered her daughter's last words.

It was during the night that Sarah heard a horse's gallop. She got up quietly not to waken her husband, grabbed her shawl and ran out. The air was cold. The ground hard with early spring frost. The sky and ground lit by the bright moon revealed the horse pawing the ground near the barn. She ran toward her. The barn door was open.

"Lyuba. Lyuba!" Sarah called into the barn frantically, but softly, breathlessly.

"Mama! Mama," a soft voice answered.

As her eyes became accustomed to the dimness of the barn, lit by the bare thread of moonlight she let in with the open door, Sarah saw Lyuba lying on a straw heap in a corner of the barn.

"Lyuba! Lyuba!" Sarah ran to her and grabbed the girl to her. She could feel the wetness on the side of Lyuba's dress, and even in the dark could see the black stain on her bodice. Sarah raised her up in her arms and rocked Lyuba sobbing.

"Who did this?" she shrieked and sobbed.

"Mama. Mama. It's all right." Lyuba said stroking her mother's head.

"I'll kill her!" Sarah shouted. "I'll kill her!"

"Sarah! Lyuba!" Yechiel stood in the doorway. His white night-clothes glowing in the dark.

"Papa!"

"Child, what has happened?" He approached the women.

"She has been shot. Go for the doctor, Yechiel! Go!" Sarah shouted. He bent over them. "Stay then," Sarah said. "Hold her and I will ride Linka—"

"No," said Lyuba. "Both of you stay with me."

Yechiel sat down next to Sarah and took his daughter's hand. The tears ran from his eyes down wrinkled cheeks into his white beard.

"Papa. You care, Papa." Lyuba whispered. "I never knew—"

"Was I so busy that you should not know?" he sobbed. He raised his face to the sky and opened his hands. "Was it in vain, God, that I loved you and prayed to you? I led a quiet life. I wrestled with your Holy Words. For what, Almighty Lord? Where are you when we need you? What evil has this child done? Why? Why?" He sobbed. Sarah pressed Lyuba closer to her. The blood seeped through Sarah's clothes, wetting her chest.

"I will kill her," Sarah muttered through her teeth.

"No. Mamushka. You can't. She was afraid, Mamushka, that's why. Live, Mamushka, Tatushka. Killing is no good. Who knows where freedom is? But live, Mama, Papa, live...."

They held her in their arms until the sun came up and then buried her.

Petrashka

PETRASHKA TIED together the greens she loved to smell, and which gave her her name, and set the little sprig of parsley in a glass on the kitchen table. She had set some aside to be used in the soup. The chicken was lying on the wooden grating, lightly salted, koshering. She had time for her brief visit to the next street in the village before it was time to wash the salt off the chicken and put it into the pot to boil. The onion, the carrot, the greens were ready for the next step.

She tied the kerchief under her neck, pushing some of the venturing gray strands under the print cotton kerchief. She would take herself down to Ruchel's house, hoping that she would find her alone, that no one would see her walking into the matchmaker's house.

Alone. So long alone had she lived in this house with her widowed mother, caring for her younger sister and brother. Lev now lived in the next town, a stonecutter. He had been apprenticed as a younger boy. Leah, her younger sister, had been the apple of everyone's eye. Adorable, pretty, smiling and singing as she lisped her baby-talk. The family revolved about her, to make her comfortable, to find her the best things to eat so she would grow strong, and the warmest clothes. The little girl slept with the mother while the older two stretched themselves out on old clothes before the stove.

As the years went by the children moved out of childhood. Boys flocked about Leah. Mother was relieved when she fell in love with a young Rabbinic student from Vilna and they were married.

Ruchel the matchmaker handled the arranging of the marriage as was the custom, especially with the head of the family gone. But Petrashka had been lost in the shuffle. Dependable, good Petrashka, no one had asked for her.

She walked down the narrow street. Fall was in the air and soon the cold would come. Leah had invited her to visit and stay to help with the second new baby coming in a few weeks.

Ruchel was in. The samovar was hot and tea was welcome. The short fast walk had exhausted Petrashka and she eagerly seized the chair Ruchel offered. She removed her kerchief as Ruchel poured the tea.

"Nu?" Petrashka asked.

"Nu—there's not much to tell."

"No hope?"

"No, don't say that," said Ruchel. "Don't even think it. But times are bad. The merchant I told you about died a few months ago, I just got word. The widower Mechel left for Odessa before I could reach him. The young man I told you about was taken into the army and will be there for five years. Meantime I want you to take back the deposit."

"No, you hold it. Something will come up. Don't you think so?"

"Sure, sure," said the matchmaker, "but I would rather the money be with you right now. If I need it, you're right here."

Ruchel went to the sewing machine drawer, unlocked it with a key, and took out a little sack with coins and brought it to Petrashka's hand.

"Take and hold it for now," she said putting the sack into her hand. Petrashka gripped the sack in her palm. Five years' work and ten years' courage were wrapped in the little sack she clutched between her fingers.

"More tea, Petrashka?" Ruchel asked.

"No. . .no, thank you. It is time for me to rinse off the salt from the chicken."

She turned back from the door for a moment.

"And the one-eyed beggar. . .he too?"

"He feels a wife would be too much responsibility."

Petrashka turned her face to the street.

The Wedding

MEEME CHANTZE was dressing when the girl rushed into her room, the only bedroom in the house, shared by the master and his wife.

"Meeme Chantze, we're going to have a wedding!"

"Wonderful. Who in the village is it?" Meeme Chantze asked, turning her head from the mirror as she braided her long golden-brown hair. Twisting it into a bun, she anchored it on the nape of her neck with large hairpins.

"Malke, the tailor's daughter," answered Luba.

"Mozel tov. A sweet girl," said Chantze. She put her winter sweater on.

"Who is the bridegroom?"

"Shmuel."

"Shmuel?"

"Shmuel, Reb Yonkel's."

"Yes, yes. I remember now," said Chantze, buttoning up to go out. "The boy lived with relatives in Moscow—to get an education."

"He didn't get much," said the maid. She began to straighten the pillows on the bed and turned to open a window speaking as she moved, "He knows as much as...well, as good as his father he'll be—but the university wouldn't look at him."

Chantze nodded her head sympathetically.

"Oy," swept out of her chest to the sky. The sigh was knit to a string of others—the whirling sighs that encompassed their lives.

"So they'll be getting married. Malkele should have a nice wedding," said Meeme Chantze.

"Without a dowry yet! What kind of wedding? Who'll come?" said Luba.

"Everybody, of course. Everyone who is invited. Who doesn't ask the whole village to such a simche—a celebration like this—to dance at their wedding? A mitzvah. What kind of person would not come?"

Later that day Malke herself came to see Meeme Chantze to invite her personally. The wedding would be soon. Not that it was a matter of urgency, but there was nothing to save in waiting. So Malkele went from one house to another inviting all the families in the village, friends, near friends and relatives. All had watched Malke grow from birth to lovely womanhood, and the village had perhaps twenty families, so with tea and cookies the greater part of the day was covered. Malke was received politely everywhere— sometimes warmly, sometimes just politely. The wedding was set for the following week. The Rabbi from Berdichev, a sister town, had already accepted the invitation to officiate. The women in town began their baking. Everyone baked. The best holiday recipes were called up, the most festive wedding strudels. Hands were slapped as they slipped under the protective cheesecloth covering pans waiting their turn outside the oven. There was mild tolerance for flies or errant fingers.

The morning of the nuptials, Luba informed Meeme Chantze that many of the villagers were not coming. Their girls had delivered their cakes and regrets.

Chaim Baer stroked his beard as he overheard the maid speaking to his wife. He was preparing to go to the mill.

"What kind of nonsense is this, Chantze?" he asked.

"It's nothing. Just people. Wait. It will work out."

"The wedding is today. It would be a terrible thing for them if people don't come," said Chaim Baer.

"Luba, take out the black satin with the beads."

"Meeme Chantze, this is only a tailor's daughter . . . your green is beautiful."

Chantze shook her beautiful head.

"I want the black—and my gold chain. Where did I put the comb I wore to Rifka's wedding in Moscow? Tell the children to put their best clothes on. We're going to a wedding in a few hours."

"Yoshe, the blacksmith tells me that Shmuel is your relative, Meeme Chantze. I didn't know you were related," Luba remarked as she laid out the black satin.

"No one can have too many relatives. We won't even worry from which side," she laughed. "After all, who is not God's child?"

Molly, her daughter-in-law, came in then.

"Meeme Chantze, can I help you dress? We are ready ourselves."

"Just button the back for me, please. Good. Thank you."

"I hear that Bayle Moskat and Frume Schochat are not coming," Molly said as she fitted the black satin loops around the small round black satin buttons which ran in a row from the back of the neck to the waist of Chantze's dress.

"Is that so?" said Chantze.

"They don't feel they have to put themselves out. The boy is only going to be a tailor."

Meeme Chantze stood still, then drew herself up in soft contemplation.

"Nu, kinderlach, let us get ready. We have a wedding to go to. Get Papa his gold watch and dust off his hat. My Sabbath scarf," she motioned to the girls.

Dressed in her black satin with tiny black beads scattered in snowflake patterns on the collar and cuffs, the back buttoned from the waist up, Chantze took the gold chain from Luba, slipped it over her head and centered it on her bosom. A handsome figure of a woman, a queen in her regal stance.

"Come, Papa," she called into the large room, "we are almost ready."

Chaim Baer strode into the room. Tall, slender, handsome with a full beard. His top hat replaced the yarmulka he usually wore in the house.

"Are you all ready children?" Meeme Chantze asked. "Come, let us go."

Chantze and Chaim led the procession to the little synagogue where the wedding tables had been set up in the square before the synagogue. And who did not follow? The entire town followed in procession. With Meeme Chantze and Fetter Chaim Baer going, if their presence graced the festivities who would stay behind? Frume buckled herself quickly into her corsets. Moshe nudged Bayle as he saw the procession going to the synagogue.

"Nu, Bayle. Don't you think we should go too? It isn't nice for us. . . ."

It was the gayest, happiest wedding the town had known in many years. And people meeting at weddings years later would nod and say, "You should have been at Malke's wedding, Malke's and Shmuel's wedding—that was something! That was a wedding to remember."

The Novitiate

AT A DISTANCE, riding down from the hills, Vasha could see Lev helping his horse pull a yoked boulder away from the quarry wall toward the center of the pit. There, clear of the other rocks, he split it dead center with his pickax. Now the horse could drag one section of the rock up the winding incline to the shed close to the mouth of the pit. There Lev would chisel the stone into a memorial tablet.

Lev steadied the horse as it ascended the narrow path bordering the pit. He looked up toward the road as he drew the horse up and released the stone from its rope.

Vasha knew Lev would be watching for him to pass on his way from the Yaraslava monastery. His seminary studies finished, newly ordained in the priesthood, Vasha Grodonsky was coming home to say his farewells to his mother and sisters before assuming his novitiate duties.

Boyhood friends, Lev and Vasha had climbed the hills and explored the fields together on their afternoons off from work or study, until Lev's father's death forced him to take over the quarry as the only Jewish stonecutter to supply the towns between Vyashaslav and Vilna. The task fell heavily on Lev's broad shoulders. The apprentice became the master, the sole support of his family and the marker of local Jewish graves.

Lev consoled himself for his abbreviated apprenticeship and his usurped dreams of another town, profession or life by marrying Marya. Marya who had given them a beautiful little girl. Pretty as pictures, both girls were. He was a happily married man.

Vasha watched Lev tilt the stone on the side with his shoulder, setting it up for the initial marking, as he guided his horse down the hill in Lev's direction. This stone might be for David Ben Zion's son. Vasha was still at home when the youth had been killed in an accident. He had been helping Max the wine merchant deliver wine for Passover when the wagon skidded on the road, overturned and crushed the boy. Lev had written him that the Rabbi from Vilna had sent word that the year would be up soon. But then Yoshe Leib's wife had died near that time, too. Lev was working hard.

Vasha moved down toward Lev and called him. Lev saw him and waved. Vasha galloped toward him on the level ground, pulled up sharply near him and leaped off his horse to embrace Lev as the dust settled around them.

"Here, sit down for a minute. Let me look at you in your new outfit." Lev smiled and sat down on a half finished tombstone, motioning Vasha to sit next to him.

"I can offer you some water, but nothing more interesting right now, I'm afraid," said Lev.

"That's all right," said Vasha settling himself on the tombstone next to Lev. "I had a large meal in Vitebsk and Mother will have a full table waiting for me." He paused. "I received your letter."

"Hope it caused you no difficulty," said Lev.

"My questions almost got me into hot water. They inquired about my sources for 'these rumors.' I almost felt like a renegade priest. I didn't want to be put out to pasture, but I wanted the truth."

"Did you get it?" asked Lev.

"I'm afraid I did some. 'Drunken peasants' was the answer."

"The priests were blameless?"

"Are you sure of your own details?" asked Vasha.

"Dead sure." Lev looked at the ground near their feet and kicked the sand. "Do you want witnesses—the dead or alive ones?"

Vasha looked at him and said, "We'll talk more about this. I must see the family. How is Marya and your little Dunya?" Vasha asked as he stood up.

"Fine," nodded Lev. Vasha could feel the unvoiced thoughts heavy on his friend's mind. Lev looked toward the house.

"Marya must be very tired not to have heard you. She will be sorry to have missed you. You know her time is almost due and she is not sleeping well at night."

Vasha reached for his horse's reins and turned to Lev once more. He looked into Lev's eyes which were on him.

"Lev do you sometimes question how I stand now, especially as a priest?"

Lev stood. He drew himself up tall and looked at Vasha's habit. He nodded before speaking, looking into his face.

"I've been wondering for months if there might be any change."

"And?"

"When I worried, when those frightening thoughts came—I prayed that I knew you as I know myself."

Vasha grabbed Lev's shoulder without looking at him, and squeezed farewell. He mounted his horse and waved as he drew his horse toward town. The sun was beginning to go down and the cool breezes began to play. He would leave Lev to mark the stone for his morning's work while the light held out.

Vasha knew that everyone had heard his horse enter the courtyard. Madame Grodonsky greeted her son with tears and cries of joy. Annitchka hugged him and sent Luba the maid to run and fetch Vera, who was picking daffodils in the fields behind the village to adorn the dinner table—all for him, the son, the firstborn, the new seminarian first grade.

"Father Gregory wrote me what a fine student you are," his mother beamed as she kissed his cheeks. "We are so proud. Your father, may God rest his soul, would have been so pleased."

"Lubitchka," she called the maid, happily, affectionately, "take the young master's jacket and dust it carefully. Go Vashinka, wash up and then eat something. Verichka is picking flowers for you. You are a little earlier than we expected. How wonderful!" She grabbed his head between her hands and kissed him again.

"I got an early start this morning," he said between kisses. "I hoped to see Father Patrovich tonight."

"Eat now." She led him into the dining room. The samovar coals were heating the water for tea. Luba brought him a basin of water and he washed his hands, dried them on the towel she presented, and said grace. The others clustered near him, each urging his favorite dish for sampling.

"More tongue? A little more lamb, Vashinka? It was a young delicious yearling."

"It was Annitchka's pet," offered Luba.

"Bah, they are all Annitchka's pets. If we listened to her we would never have a chicken or any meat to eat. They are all pets," laughed Madame Grodonsky. "My tender-hearted Annitchka." She leaned over and kissed her daughter's forehead as they all sat around the table watching Vasha.

Vasha ate slowly, contemplatively. He wanted to speak with his mother alone and he felt that she realized this. As Luba brought in second helpings of pudding and cake, Madame Grodonsky chased the others from the table, even Verichka, who had stealthily entered while Vasha was eating and tickled him behind the ear with the daffodils before kissing him and proceeding to decorate the table with the wild young yellow flowers of springtime.

"Go, go! I want a few minutes with the boy. It's a mother's privilege. I haven't seen him for six months—go, go, wait for us in the sitting room." She embraced each of her daughters and moved them toward the door. When they were alone she turned to her son.

"Vashinka, something is troubling you. I can tell by the way you've knit your right brow."

Vasha laughed, "You think so, Mother? How well you know me. But since you've asked me, Matushka, what is this new business I hear with the Jews?"

"Which business and why should it concern you? How?"

"Matushka, I took the cloth because I believed in the goodness of people and because I want to help them."

"Jews?"

"Jews too—they are our brethren you know."

"We have had a few good ones in town, but still my boy they rejected the Lord. They are Christ-killers."

"Mother, I don't want to discuss history or theology with you right now. But if we are Christians in the true sense of the word in following the teachings of Him who died for us, for our sins, shouldn't we also follow his teachings of forgiveness? What happened two thousand years ago is not as important as what is happening now."

"Vashinka, that must border on blasphemy! What you are saying!"

"I think not mother. I must know. I must understand how the good Christian justifies brutality and murder to himself."

"You heard about Vilna?"

"Yes—a little. It is true then?"

She shook her head. "True."

She looked at him. He could see she was tying her thoughts together for argument.

"But you must save men's souls, not worry about their bodies. After all, life is a trial and suffering for us to endure. . . ."

"So we should help the Jews suffer a little more. Do you think our Lord prescribed this?"

Madame Grodonsky shook her shoulders. "Patrovich says the good Jews became Christians at the death of our Lord. Those that were left were the wicked ones doomed to eternal punishment in this world and the next for their blindness, their unwillingness to follow the good life set down by our Lord Jesus Christ." She crossed herself.

"Isn't it funny, Mother, that I find nothing in our Lord's testament that tells us that we must murder or plunder Jews. Perhaps I have read too much of Voltaire and Rousseau and Lessing to accept everything without question. You will quote me Paul and I will quote you Peter. These are not new arguments for me. I've had them countless times with my fellow novices. They seem to blind themselves to the written word and interpret in a way to suit themselves." And others, he added under his breath.

He stared at the tablecloth, playing with a lump of sugar that his mother had laid there for his tea. He watched his mother's eyes. If she only knew how often he had had self-doubts—about the Jews—but always he argued himself back to this stance with reason and feeling. On those occasions, when he had no ready answers yet, no biblical references or facts at his fingertips, silently he had crawled into himself in helpless embarrassment. He felt ashamed of those moments now that he had beaten down his own doubts and felt he knew where right lay. He found the truth where it lay long buried under the ritual of unthought word and unquestioned doctrine.

Vasha felt his mother's eyes on him as he realized that he had lapsed into his own thoughts and had closed her off from them. He looked up at her, into her eyes intent on his face, and picked up the thread of their conversation.

"Six days ago five hundred Jews were killed in a few hours," he said. "I was supposed to leave for Vilna last week and Father Zagrov asked that I stay and do some additional work for him and Father Gregory and gave me early leave to go home instead. That's when I wrote that I would be home." He rubbed his forehead hard with the palm of his hand. "There is something wrong when men can rationalize their ulterior desires and foul motives into acts of righteousness—wrong when goodness is an excuse for brutality, and the easy absolution of the sinner, of the brutal evil doer...."

He remembered pondering these thoughts as a philosophy student in Moscow before becoming interested in the clergy or, indeed, before he felt that the church would be his way to help people, to inform and bring them to a better way of living, of finding God and the divine in themselves. The hope he had for mankind—the goodness of the sky and the earth and all it offered. How good it was just to be alive.

Matushka pushed more pirogi toward him and Annitchka slipped in and put some marmelade near his cup for his tea. He drank the tea slowly. It was steaming and delicious. He enjoyed being home and the mother-love-laden meal, but he wanted to get to Lev's before it was too late in the evening.

Last year he spent many hours with Marya and Lev playing with little Dunya. Sweet little blue-eyed dumpling of a baby. Bright. Only a year old then. She played with him as he offered her the fingers of his hands to grasp, going into spasms of giggles when she caught one of his fingers. Blonde, sweet-smelling little head of soft curls with pink baby skin showing through the fine golden strands.

And he wanted to visit Father Patrovich. He would find him either at home or at the church, even at this late hour. They had not seen eye to eye on several issues last year when they discussed the village and some points of theology. The disagreement was tempered by Olga Patrovich's cakes and freshly brewed tea.

They had sat near the samovar half that day trying not to disagree on the fundamental and essential matters. The preaching of the crucifixion and the condemnation of the Jews were philoso-phized over. Patrovich could almost be rational, and even voiced sympathies when Vasha brought up the bloody history of the Jew in Russia.

"So after the horrors of forced baptism and forced conscriptions, for a brief while in the early part of the reign of Alexander I, a more liberal monarch than Russia had known until then, some of the restrictions were lifted. Jews could even enter the universities. But that was for a very short time, just a few years." So Vasha had spoken, in a text-like narrative. "After these few years again the Jews were milked and killed, whole populations were expelled from the cities to die of cold and starvation. Truly a long history of terror and abuse."

Vasha had hoped to appeal to Patrovich's reason by these narrations. To make him aware of the Jew as a human being.

"Alas, too true, perhaps," said Patrovich, after listening politely to Vasha. "Some Russians are mercenary. We are having trouble with our own brethren. Last month the monks from the Papist church broke two of our windows, but our boys bloodied up their noses. Vatican vermin—the traitors!"

Patrovich had proceeded to harangue his brothers in Rome for half an hour without pause. The grievances poured out: they were inexecrable demons, men without souls or hearts—butchers. Bolsheviks to the cause of the church. His head shook and his beard trembled with indignation. Vasha had recalled this hostiity from his own childhood, when the house maids walking him past the Catholic church would raise their fists toward it and spit.

The essence of the division of the churches escaped Vasha. Papal doctrine claimed that the spirit came from the Son in trinitarian doctrine. Russian orthodoxy claimed it from the Father. In essence a whole. In practice a division. Did it matter how a man was to be dissected if dissection were the goal? Or how a wound is repaired if stitching is required? Does one begin to build a house from the northern or southern corners, or the eastern or western, all directions given their due?

This year, as last, Olga Patrovich was prepared for Vasha's visit. She had met Madame Grodonsky in the market that morning and was alerted to Vasha's early return.

"Have some more cakes with your tea," she urged, moving the tray on the table closer to Vasha. She smiled at him expectantly and he couldn't refuse another kuchen. He lifted the crumbling soft cake and carried it to his mouth. Filled with raspberry jam, deliciously fresh and still warm. He smiled his thanks with a full mouth. Olga Patrovich beamed.

"Tell us something about your studies at the seminary," urged Patrovich, shaking his capped head. "It's been a long time since mine."

Patrovich had been at the seminary for a very short time—a briefing and a few classes, then an apprenticeship to a local priest to learn the prayers by heart. Both knew he was a lay cleric of peasant stock that the church frequently admitted, not being able to service the Russian masses with the trained University theologians the population needed.

There was light response to the clergy's call these days. New professions were being formed, new ideologies expounded. Science had opened borders and people were looking for ways to cross them. A new age of enlightenment was felt and nourished periodically at the universities, too frequently watched and buckled under czarist decree.

Vasha wanted to ask Patrovich some direct questions relating to the Jews of Vyashaslav, but didn't know how to broach them. Not sure how the priest was disposed he groped for neutral ground, the government. But still it burst out bluntly as, "Do you know what are the latest decrees about the Jews from Petersburg? I understand there was a terrible pogrom in Vilna."

The priest looked at him and scratched his head under his cap.

"Mmmm—not much change—some aid can be given, but cautiously."

"Cautiously? Why?"

"A few can be protected."

"Why only a few?"

"The Czar feels that we have quite a few too many. More than we need, and purges are healthy for the populace. For the few, it is to show...well, there is some Rothchild money that has been offered, and the Czar would like that too."

Vasha felt sick. The cake he was eating lay heavy on his tongue and he couldn't spit it out without offending his host.

"Why is this necessary? I can't believe it." His voice shook.

Patrovich looked puzzled at Vasha's response. Uncomprehending that Vasha's thoughts could differ from his, from the accepted views of the time.

"Do you think it is right to kill Jews, Patrovich?" Vasha asked point blank, looking into the older priest's eyes.

"If the government says so, is there an alternative?" said the man, shrugging his shoulder. The black habit absorbed the shadows, making the priest look larger than he was.

"Is this ethically, morally, right? Answer as a Christian! Is this right?"

"According to Paul they are to be scourged...."

"And according to Christ, if they are guilty—I say 'if'—they are to be forgiven. As a man of the cloth are you going to let them be slaughtered?"

Patrovich opened his hands, "I will do what I can. More tea, Olga, please!"

Vasha left the Patrovich house shortly for the stone cutter's cottage. He would write to Father Gegory in the Yaraslava monastery. It was quite dark, but by the moonlight Vasha could see the outline of the granite quarry as he ascended the slight incline which led to the cottage.

The light shone from the cottage window, smoke was coming from the chimney. Marya was cooking dinner or fixing tea. Lev was a large man and sometimes liked a snack before going to bed. Marya. Marya, the prettiest girl he had ever known. Even his mother had remarked on her fine features and small hands, "Very ladylike for a Jewess."

Vasha tied his horse to a tree and walked up the sloping path to the cottage, crunching granite chips under his feet. His habit sweeping against the isolated low bush next to the stone-cutting shed which faced the house. Vasha knocked on the door. Lev opened it with a broadening smile as he recognized him.

"Look who's here, Marya—set a place at the table. It's Vasha! I told you he was back from the seminary for a few days...I hope," he added, looking questioningly at Vasha.

"A few more days," said Vasha, smiling at both of them. "It's good to be back. Where's Dunya?" he asked, looking about the room.

Marya, standing near the stove, answered him as she stirred the pot quickly and dried her hands to greet him.

"She hasn't been feeling so good these last two days. A bit of fever—we hope it's nothing. The doctor was here today and says it might be diptheria. You know there are a few cases in Pajalitz. He said to watch her and call him immediately if she shows any difficulty in breathing. I'll bring her in as soon as she wakes up. You won't recognize her—a regular young lady. Come sit down. Lev, give Vasha the big chair with the cushion."

"Sure, sure," said Lev, bringing up the chair to the table. "The others have nails coming through in spots. I was supposed to fix them." He winked at Vasha guiltily, avoiding Marya's eyes.

"I'm glad you remembered." She laughed and shook the soup ladle at him. "At least you remembered what I had asked you to do. How he avoids doing what he doesn't want to! My royal procrastinator! But you should see the swing he made for Dunya! That he worked on like a Cossack!"

"Come sit down." Lev pushed Vasha toward the chair impatiently. "There is so much I want to talk to you about."

Lev moved another chair to the table and sat opposite Vasha. Marya brought two steaming bowls to the table.

"Warmed over borsht tonight," she said as she set one bowl in front of Vasha and the other before Lev. "I hope I didn't make it too sweet."

Vasha took the spoon she handed him and put it into the borsht. It smelled so good. He smiled his thanks to her and wondered what people would think if they knew he was here. His mother, he was afraid, would not approve of his visit, though she knew of his boyhood friendship with Lev. She had tried to discourage it, diverting his activities to include other Russian boys. But after school he always found time to speak with Lev.

They would wander off into the meadow behind the old synagogue, the meadow filled with yellow daffodils. There they would ponder the mysteries of the earth, the sky, and all being. They would pluck a few daffodils to bring home for the dinner table, enjoying their beauty, but reluctant to take their tender lives, a sacrifice to man's aesthetic needs. They would talk about God and feel close to Him on the hilltop. And Vasha felt that Lev understood what he felt as no Christian boy he knew.

And Lev would tell him about the old testament and the interpretations of the Laws. And his God had the same feeling toward life that Vasha was learning. That life was sacred. Lev had talked to him at times of the history of the Jews, the massacres in the middle ages. How the Jews were chased from one land to another—killed, tortured, enslaved.

He told Vasha what his grandfather had told him of the good czars and the cruel ones. Sometimes one would let the Jews lift their heads for a while, and under others they were lower than serfs and animals. They were not treated as human. Only when the Jews had the temple in Jerusalem were they at peace—free. Why did this have to be so? Lev would raise his head to the sky and ask Vasha. And Vasha would think and not answer.

"You have something on your mind I see," Lev said. Vasha looked up from the borsht and into Lev's eyes.

"I do have something on my mind."

"You know about the Vilna pogrom?"

"I've heard."

"What do you think is going to be?" Lev asked softly, not anxious for Marya to catch this drift of conversation.

"I don't know. I wanted to talk to you about that," said Vasha.

Marya set three cups of tea on the table and sat down with them.

"Some sugar, Vasha?" She offered him a few lumps.

"Thank you, Marya." He took them from her hand.

Suddenly from behind the curtained-off area in one of the rooms came a baby's cry. Marya jumped up and went to it. In a minute she brought back a flushed, tear-swept Dunya rubbing her eyes in the light. Dunya recognized her father and extended her arms toward

him. Lev took her and sat her in her in his lap. Dunya looked at
Vasha. He smiled at her but she clutched her father tighter.

"You can tell the child is still sick," said Vasha. "Perhaps Dr.
Oblensky should see her again tonight."

Marya went over to the child and felt Dunya's head with her
hand. "She actually feels cooler than when I laid her down. She
seems to be breathing without difficulty. What do you say, Lev?"

"She seems a little better now. We're not going to sleep yet.
We'll watch. I can be at Dr. Oblensky's in five minutes."

Marya took a half-willing Dunya from her father's arms and
went to put her back to bed.

"So Vasha, you've heard of some things with the pogrom?" Lev
asked.

"Yes. And I'm going to write to Yaraslav tonight. I hope I am
not too late to find out more...if it will help."

"You expect more of these?"

"I'm afraid so, Lev."

"We are too. We know of the new edicts from Moscow and
Petersburg. It doesn't look good...for us." He chewed on his
lower lip and drank his tea. "What to do. What to do," he chanted
to himself so low Vasha could hardly pick up the words.

"What's best?" He turned toward Vasha. "To go to the city now
is not so smart...and you never know who will turn against you
here. There are no gypsies around to hide us now—the Czar has
exiled and exterminated them. We are next."

"I have spoken to Patrovich about this," said Vasha.

"Yes?"

"In case of emergency I think you'll be able to trust him."

"Better than your mother?"

Vasha nodded.

"But after some of his sermons, I wonder."

"I'm going to talk to him about you, and unless I get word to you
to the contrary, you will be able to find refuge with him—this
time."

"You expect. . .?" Lev stirred.

"I honestly don't know what to expect." Vasha looked at his friends. Marya had lulled Dunya back to sleep and was helping herself to a warmer cup of tea. She refilled all their cups. They finished their tea in silence and Vasha left.

Vasha wrote that night and posted the letter early the next day. He wanted answers from Yaraslav. He had no connections closer to the Czar and the church seemed to be the source of information seeping to the peasantry.

Two days later a man drove in from Pajolitz to warn the Jewish population of the village that the pogromchikis—the White soldiers—had hit Pajolitz. He was a peddler from another town on his way to deliver goods to a tailor in Pajolitz when he saw the soldiers chasing Jews out of their houses. He left and drove here to Vyashaslav, the closest town. He was leaving for the hills. He warned the stone-cutter to carry the news to the rest of the town and in panic left.

It was then, Lev later told Vasha, that they decided to act upon his advice and seek refuge with the priest and his wife. Especially since that day Lev had not borrowed the horse and they could not move far and fast with the baby. Several Jews had found their way into the basements of the Patrovich's house looking for safety in the sanctity of the church grounds, hoping that their local priest would not be one of those to turn them over to the pogromchikis. One heard all kinds of stories.

They told Vasha that when Dunya began to cry, Marya realized that the child had not yet been fed that morning. She herself could do without, but she felt that she could ask Madame Patrovich for something for Dunya. Which she did. Madame Patrovich said she would find something for the child and soon returned with a bit of pork. Marya fed the forbidden food to Dunya. In such instances the transgression is forgiven. Lev reassured her that the woman was not vicious, only ignorant perhaps, but Marya held to her feelings, as she narrated the incident to Vasha when he came for them. He had been through the town checking.

Vasha found the old shamus in his make-shift synagogue
quarters, which served as a school for the few young Jewish
children in the town and for services, and which was mainly the
storage depot for the wine merchant's kegs. The old man was
encsconced in the oven which housed him for the night. It had only
been a small band of roving soldiers, and everyone was safe. Many
had spent the night in the woods.

Vasha returned with Marya and Lev to their cottage.

"I don't like the looks of things," he told them, "and I'm afraid
you may not be able to trust the priest any longer."

"You've heard something?" asked Lev.

"Not yet. It's something I feel. I can't explain it."

Vasha had tea with them and left to return to his home.

As he ate his lunch he felt his mother's eyes on him. He knew
she sensed his disturbance, his anguish. Unfortunately, she didn't
share it or understand it. He couldn't even discuss it with her. A
Jew was not a human thing to her, for all her kindness and
goodness of heart. For all her reverence for human life. She cried
when Bulya their favorite cow broke her back and had to be killed.
She wept with every groan of the gentle creature. But where a Jew
was concerned—apathy? No. Violence. A hidden hate seeping up
through two thousand years, festering, nourished by two thousand
years of teaching—of church teachings, forgetting the human code
set by the Lord. The church made its own.

He felt that she knew what was on his mind and was unable or
unwilling to broach it. He looked at her and saw fear in her eyes.
She was worried about him, too. Poor Matushka.

Vasha visited Marya and Lev before dawn the next morning. No
letter had come yet from Yaraslav and he was beginning to wonder
if it would help much. The new edicts were being posted in the
towns. Jews were being forced to sell their businesses for next to
nothing—the puny rights of ownership they had garnered in
twenty years were being abrogated.

"If you hear or see anything suspicious run to the hills," Vasha
told them. "As a matter of fact, it might not be a bad idea to go

there for a few days." He urged them to take mattresses and warm clothing and hide in the woods on the hillsides, "for a few days anyhow."

"You think it's that bad?" said Lev.

"Yes. After Pajolitz, I'm afraid it's too close. If you have friends in Kiev, perhaps that would be wise. I don't know. The news from the cities is not good either. There have been many arrests and shootings. The government troops rampaged through a Jewish section outside of Petersburg and killed hundreds. What can I say? What advice can I give? Can anyone?"

He opened his hands to heaven and then bent over a large half-finished tombstone as in pain.

Lev moved toward him. Vasha was crying. Softly he sobbed, helpless, despairing. He reached a hand out to Lev, drying his tears with the other. He smiled at Marya standing near the cottage door. He could see that she was embarrassed for him and smiled to reassure her. It did not distress him to let his friends see his tears. They said their farewells.

At home Vasha found a letter waiting for him. The Yaraslava superior had been forwarded his letter and the response was brief. "Return for further orders." This was the answer he had put so much hope in.

That was Saturday. Sunday he heard from Luba the maid that Patrovich had read an edict from the pulpit. New government regulations concerning the Jews. Their homes and their positions were now available to the local peasants. They need only come to him to discuss this and file their claim. Land the Jews had never been permitted to own, but their little shops, the mills, the quarry. . . .

Vasha thought Lev and Marya would have to leave, and he knew Lev had been working very little lately. There was hardly enough money for the living, much less for obeisance to the dead.

The next day Vasha slept late. He had been troubled by dreams all night. Countless times he had gone over in his mind what he would say to the prelate. He had marked the chapters he would quote from the new testament. In this way he would plead the cause of his brethren the Jews, and point out the errors of hate. He woke with Luba knocking at the door.

"Look out the window, young master, the White soldiers are here to save Mother Russia from the Jews." She knelt near the window and crossed herself. He ran to the window. Coming down the road was a column of soldiers. Marching and chanting at their head was Patrovich and the local Roman Catholic priest carrying the large crucifixes from their church altars.

"Kill the Jews!" the priests were chanting, and the soldiers echoing the words. Vasha threw on his habit as he ran out of the house toward them. He flung himself on Patrovich.

"Stop! What are you doing?" Vasha screamed.

Patrovich stopped his chanting as Vasha grabbed him and wrestled with him for the crucifix. They continued moving forward, pushed on by the weight of the column behind them.

"Dear Vasha, let us pass," Patrovich said, calmly gripping the crucifix.

"Come join us!" said the Catholic priest. "We are only doing God's work."

"This young man has other ideas, I believe; I don't think he'll be much help to us," said Patrovich, disengaging Vasha's hands from the crucifix and pushing him aside. "I don't think he'll be a priest long...a little crazy perhaps, too friendly with the Jews and they poisoned his mind. Come soldiers of God and the Czar! Come to the church for the blessing now that you have cleansed Russia!"

Vasha, pushed away by the column of moving men, now saw the soldiers as they passed by him bespattered with blood, clutching uncleaned wet sabers, exultant after battle.

He ran toward the quarry. He ran breathless over the field and tore his habit off to run unencumbered. Everything was still when he came to the quarry. His heart beat with fright. He ran into the house calling for Marya and Lev. Behind the torn curtain he found Dunya dead in her crib, her head almost severed from her body. He ran out without touching her. In the shed were blood stains leading to the quarry. Two bodies lay there. He leaped down the incline. Marya stripped naked lay dead. Her belly ripped open, a mangled foetus between her spread legs. Her open eyes on the sky. Blood everywhere. He turned to Lev lying face down and gasped. His arms had been cut off at the shoulders. He turned him over and gasped. His eyes had been punctured. He was still alive.

"Lev!" Vasha cried and held him in his arms and rocked him.

"Vasha, Vashinka" Lev recognized his voice, "What's left?"

Vasha could only grip him and cry.

"They came upon us so quickly we couldn't run. Marya was taken to the shed. I heard her cry many times. Many times. Build us the temple in Jerusalem, Oh, God. Oh, God make us free! Make us free!"

Vasha held him until he died and then flung himself on the rocks with the pickax Lev would have defended himself with. He hacked away at the granite. He tore at the rocks.

"Lev! Lev!" he would call out once in a while. "I will help you build the temple in Jerusalem. You will see. You will see, Lev!"

Summer's Idyll

THE RUSSIAN sun sparked the air, warming the earth as Sonya dangled her feet in the cold little brook. She smoothed her skirt over her knees and over the splintered boards of the narrow bridge. In a little while she hoped Peter would come by on his way back to the village. The sun was high in the sky, filtering softly through the high tops of the trees. The wind blew softly, disturbing nothing, not even the spring-warmed air. In the distance the cow bells clanked as the cows made their lazy way through the meadow. The water moved coldly and quietly about her ankles. The pebbles blinked beneath the ripples.

Yesterday, at this time, Peter had stopped and talked to her for almost an hour. They had laughed together and talked about the villagers...Ruchel's one-horned goat had gotten himself jammed between two trees chasing the children who had been teasing him—the cat who had kittened in the synagogue under the ark, to the consternation of the early Sabbath worshippers, holding up the service until the shamus brought her warm milk to quiet the loud insistent mewing.

Sonya blushed with embarrassment as she remembered her encounter with Peter a few weeks ago. Max, her husband, was walking fast a few feet before her, turning toward her every few feet to berate her. She had forgotten the hours in the field while gathering daffodils; forgotten the Sabbath dinner and Max's impatience if it were delayed beyond sunset, when he came home from the Friday evening service. Usually kind, he was in a foul mood lately, and arguing would have been in vain. It was easier to follow quietly keeping her eyes on her feet as she walked after him, in her hand the guilty daffodils swinging bravely yellow in easy walking cadence. Sonya looked at the loose stones under her feet as she followed Max, eyes to the ground knowing the direction to the house blindly.

She knew how Max hurried home from work Friday evenings. He worked for a wine merchant, taking orders and delivering cases of wine to neighboring towns, some exhaustingly distant. He was extremely impatient now, for there had been very few times in the seven years they had been married, that she had been unprepared for the Sabbath meal. Once she had been helping a neighbor care for a very ill child, and once when she herself had miscarried. And Max had always been kind to her—especially then.

Gently Sonia kicked ripples in the brook with her toes. Yesterday morning she had sat at the table with Malke Raize the widow. Malke put poppy seed cakes out for them to enjoy with their tea, and sat there with her gray hair framing what was still a jovial face, round, full of sport and laughter.

Malke had spent all her life with one man who, according to Malke, never danced or made enough money to keep worry away. The years of her life had crept away. Shimmen was dead: now she sewed for the village—and meager that was. There were few fancy ladies who needed a seamstress or occasions warranting such splendor. Now and then a wedding—a new flounce to be added to the redone or borrowed bridal dress. Oftimes a shroud—two pieces of cloth sewn down the sides, a short bit of work for her. Remarriage? Who? When? No one came. No one asked. Her two children—grown—lived in their cities. She was sometimes called upon when a new baby came.

Sonya felt her own life was ebbing away. Drifting in dull monotony, the sameness of routine, the lack of adventure—of going and seeing. She could have a new dress when she needed or wanted one. But she too, like Malke, wanted someone to dance with, to be young with, to be happy with and make the memories that later would sweeten a widow's tea. She could feel Max's approval of her fine dinner or particularly sweet-smelling var-nichkes by his gentle touch on the back of her neck or head—at night it assumed a masculine thrust.

Once, in an expansive Sabbath mood, Max let drop to Sonya how he—shy and reticent as he was—came to be led under the marriage canopy. He had been walking the Rabbi home after a Sabbath morning service, and as he turned to continue his way to his own house, the Rabbi had tugged him quickly at his sleeve.

"Max, why is it that you are not married yet? You have a nice little house—make a decent living. It isn't fitting for a Jew of your age to continue to live his life alone and leave no children behind."

The Rabbi's bright questioning eyes looked into Max's face. Max shrugged.

"Rabbi, I really hadn't thought of it."

"A man must think of more than work. Time is seeping by slowly, Max. It isn't right—a good pious man like you—at least you should see that there is a son to say kaddish after you."

So shortly afterwards, in considering the available marriageable girls in the village, Max settled on Sonya. She was only fifteen when her widowed father was informed of Max's interest and made her marriage arrangement. Max was dependable, honest, and had a little money put aside, and Sonya was a good daughter. Her father lived with them until his death four years ago.

Sonya felt that Max had many misgivings later, whether he had done the right thing in marrying her. To him she might appear sweetly docile and lovely, but she thought he often seemed plagued, perhaps wondering if he were equal to assuming the responsibility for another human's life and happiness. She tried to seem happy— she never complained. But he seemed helpless in communicating with her, as he was with children and other women. They seemed to be in different worlds, and as one could not understand or participate in the world of children, he humored women or treated them with a particle of difference, since in all fairness she knew they could not be invited into the adult male world. Assuming this, and a woman's ignorance of the study of Talmud, Sonya felt that Max could never invite her to share or help with any question that might arise in his mind as he studied the holy books at night—the books he poured over after he had eaten and checked off his day's accounts and receipts for orders for the delivery of wine. Sometimes he would ask her to hold the ledger as he read off the numbers, tallying figures as the monthly accounts were readied.

She would meet his puzzled glance if she looked over his shoulder at the talmudic text, briefly puzzled and perhaps imposed upon, before she saw his thoughts recede as he returned his glance to the page. She felt that he minimized or totally forgot that among her assets was her ability to read and write—and think. Useless assets for a woman, perhaps. But her father had once found her a bright obedient pupil, and since there was no son in the family, had taught her.

During the week, because of Max's late deliveries, Sonya ate her meals alone, sometimes reading during the meal, or picking up a borrowed book or newspaper, she dallied leisurely enjoying her tea after supper.

On Friday evenings, Sonya usually had the Sabbath meal on the table long before Max arrived. And on these evenings, as always, Max would read during the meal. Sonya would feed him one course after another, as he finished each, never removing his eyes from the printed page, one hand on the fork, the other holding the book flat. He cut his meat with the fork's edge, grumbling if the piece were too tough and he had to use a knife. Then he would put the napkin on the page to hold his place, slice several pieces of meat and resume his reading.

Sonya watched to see when each dish was finished. Sometimes a forkful would be suspended in mid-air as his eyes traced the words down the page and would almost miss his mouth. He was neat in spite of his absorption, and only occasionally would a grease spot appear on the book or tablecloth. Sometimes she wished he would talk to her. Eventually she gave up even wishing that.

Lonely at those times, she hoped, as she knew Max did so urgently, for another to share their life with, but another pregnancy had not occurred. Max looked at her beggingly, asking, hoping, each month, but there was no change in her physical condition. Each month she went through the ritual cleansing bath. He was angry with her she felt.

"Scatterbrained!" Max had yelled at her as they walked through the village streets toward their house. Sonya had glanced up for a moment when Max was sullenly silent and saw Peter's eyes on her as she and Max continued walking. Just a glance. His eye engaged hers for a swift minute and she walked on. Her eyes on the guilty daffodils which were to grace the dinner table.

Not many years ago she would often find Peter's eyes on her as she and her friends ran toward the fields to gather blackberries in their aprons. He would be wrestling with young men in the field behind the school yard, playing before they went to work or study. Once when they were very young he had talked to her when he and his friends were pushed near her and her father by the crowd attending Simchas Torah services in the synagogue. Peter found a seat near them on the benches and her father helped him fix his apple on his flag. They laughed when the apple split and toppled into Peter's hand and he began to eat it. She had attended his Hebrew class for a while when her father had specifically asked the Rabbi to instruct her along with his regular students. She was the only one who prepared her lessons.

Suddenly it ended—she became a woman—the town spoke of her betrothal to Max, the wine merchant from Vitebsk. Soon she was not to be with the young girls weaving flowers in their hair—chewing bucksaw as they walked arm in arm along the village creek in the spring.

Suddenly Sonya was startled by sounds of brush moving as she sat on the bridge planks watching the water flow under the bridge. Someone was coming through the bushes. A dog's head appeared.

"Here Pushka!" she laughed. She fondled the dog's head as he nuzzled her skirt. Peter would be close behind. She heard his steps but kept her head bent toward the dog.

"Good day, Sonya," Peter called as he came closer to the bridge, taking the familiar worn dusty road rather than Pushka's shortcut. The fine dust spray preceded his feet. He stopped near Sonya. She looked up with a hesitant half-smile that she felt wanted to broaden itself as she looked at his battered hat half on his head, sun blonde, tanned, his flecked bluish-green eyes sparkled with his smile. Flecks of dust sat near his nostrils and she could see the sweat rings on the shirt under his armpits as his broad shoulders shielded the hot sun as he stood over her, leaning on the handle of his scythe. A tall straight young man, with thick strong muscle under his sweaty shirt.

"Beautiful day, isn't it?" she asked the smiling face.

"It sure is. But I would prefer it a little cooler for working." He wiped his brow, lay his scythe down and sat down near her on the wooden planks. Flies buzzed in the silence.

"How have things really been for you?" he asked quietly.

"All right." Still embarrassed by the memory of the scene in the village street, she added, "Max is really very good to me."

"Why shouldn't he be? You're very pretty, you know?"

She said nothing and looked up to meet his eyes. He leaned his tanned face closer to hers; she felt their shoulders touch.

"Very pretty," he said.

She held his eyes and knew as he moved his head toward her that his lips would find hers. She felt his arm slip behind her back and tighten, drawing her closer to him. When he released her, she was breathless and he flushed. He rubbed his nose against her cheek and pressed his face against hers.

"You're so soft, so silky soft—and so beautiful." His hand crept up to her bosom and cupped it gently—she didn't want to remove it. He kissed her neck and reached for one of her hands.

"You have such pretty little hands, pretty—sweet," he murmered into her hair as he drew her closer. Held to him she felt his breath on her cheek as her head rested on his chest. She felt his hand firm on her breast. Suddenly she was aware of the sun's movement in the sky. She lifted her face from his chest.

"I must be going—it's getting late." She swept out of his arms. Feeling his eyes on her, she got up, picked up her shoes near the bridge—she saw him wave as she darted a smile toward him and ran.

Sonya sang lightly as she set the table that evening. When Max came home, she heard from him that the Czar's soldiers had been in the village that day looking for conscripts. A neighbor had already told her that Peter's mother was arranging a good hiding place for him with the gypsies camped nearby. They would be on the alert.

Fortunately the soldiers had not combed the fields that day looking for available able-bodied Jewish males. Rachmiel Zedek had had his little son ruptured earlier that year to avoid his ever being called into the Czar's service. Jacob Ben Favish, years ago, had blinded himself in one eye. The Jews had a bad time of it in the Czar's army. If they weren't killed by the enemy, the Russian soldiers would often shoot them in the back.

Sonja retired early that night and thought of Peter when Max made love to her.

The next day Sonya found herself drifting toward the little bridge, detouring from the well with her water bucket. No sign of Peter. She walked through town looking for a glimpse of him or his mother, and seeing his mother, waited for others to ask her about her son. She was afraid her questioning would give her away. People were staying in their homes apprehensive and troubled. If the Czar's quota was not met by the village, who knew who could be taken off the streets and marched off?

With the oncoming Passover, Max would be out until after dark each night as he made his trips to the outlying districts. So toward evening of the next day Sonya found herself rushing back to the bridge. Peter was sitting on the bridge. Pushka lay near him. She saw him stand up when he saw her—and she rushed into his arms.

"I was so afraid for you, Peter!" She hugged him to her, "The soldiers were by."

"Darling. My sweet, sweet darling," he kissed her, brushed the hair from her face and sat down pulling her down into his lap, and putting his face against her breast.

"Your heart is beating so fast," he said, and kissed her breast through her dress. She held his head tight against her, not wanting to let him go—keeping his head and the moment tight to her, within her.

"Peter, I'm so afraid for you—so afraid," she said over and over between his kisses.

"I'll be all right. Always could take care of myself," he insisted finally.

She smiled as she remembered hearing once of peasant children ambushing him and a group of boys coming home from Hebrew school—the villagers still talked about the beating he gave those little rogues. After a few such incidents, Peter became a tough scrapper and could hold his own with any bully, though he had been a very shy boy when he first moved to the village with his newly widowed mother to live on the charity of their father's cousin, the village butcher.

They held each other in silence. The fear thick about them. The woods greened darker near them in the shifting sunlight. The meadow lay velvety golden in front of them. She felt Peter lift her up tenderly and walk her past the sunhazed grassy meadow deeper into the woods, into the warm shade of elms.

He held her on his knees and fondled her breasts inside her dress, and then laid her gently down on the soft earth. She felt him lift her unresisting dress and slowly caress her thighs. She knew her skin was soft under the touch of his strong, calloused fingers. He kissed her cheek, then her mouth; she looked into his eyes and closed hers dreamily. She was warm with happiness, feeling his awareness of her womanhood and his pleasure in it. She felt her body eagerly waiting, wanting and warmly opening to receive him, and she felt him man in her.

They parted that night, planning, hoping to meet again, whenever they could. She returned home and he to the gypsy camp.

Each evening she walked by the bridge and waited. By his mother's tears a few days later, she knew that he had been found and taken to fill the village quota. With quiet despair she listened avidly to anyone bringing news of the conscripts from the village. They heard of a push toward the Austrian border. A few weeks later news of Peter's death was received. With difficulty Sonya attended the special service the Rabbi held in his memory. There in the synagogue she could blend her tears with those of the congregation. At this time, after she missed her second period, Sonya knew she was pregnant.

Everyday she would stop at the bridge and feel her stomach. She would teach this one to say the kaddish, the prayer for the dead, for his father.

Village of the Maimed

ZISA SAT BY the window watching the birds whirl in circles ellipsing the blue sky as they gathered in preparation for their journey south. South. She had heard about the southlands. Warm. Fruit trees bore all year she had been told. The vines no sooner ripened and picked would begin budding again. And the blossoms! She was told that the warm air of those lands were always fragrant. And the soft winds carried the fragrances even into the cities of these blessed areas.

She could only dream. She would never see such a country. Zisa looked down at her twisted foot. Such a distance was not for walking and who could afford a wagon ride? The village would weather its winters and summers. Rags would be changed for newer rags. No one had money. The village scratched its existence from the fields and sides of the mountains. Which villager would not give good years of his life to see warmer happier lands?

Yesterday or last year the village thrived. Chickens and goats ran freely through its streets. Plump, well-fed as most of the inhabitants. In the winter the cellar's wheat and potatoes would see them through until the hard cold ground thawed and could be broken by the spade and reseeded, when the ice broke and spring water ran again.

The birds grew in numbers as they gathered. The circles enlarged shaping into spear-headed triangles, streaked across the sky to settle again, chattering, flapping, anxious to be gone. The wind rustled the ready-to-drop leaves of the trees housing these noisy guests.

Her hands idle, Zisa observed the noiseless interim between the trial flights. There was no one to sew for as she had before. Close work, true. But it paid. And she loved the pretty things she embroidered for others to wear at festivals and weddings. Weddings. Her own had been planned not so long ago. She would walk over the hillock with her friend Sonja to look for her bridegroom when he came from the fields or walked to the synagogue.

They would grip the wild brambles to steady themselves on their ascent and slide giggling into the dust when they missed their footing. Zisa rubbed her rigid, frozen, twisted foot. Numb. It dragged when she walked, indenting the earth.

No one had been prepared for the attack. They had talked about pogroms heard about remotely from far. The tall mountains buffered them from the rest of the world. And of what value was a poor village? There was no overabundance. Their livestock was barely enough to support them, and perhaps for a rare occasion provide them with a small luxury brought by a passing peddler— soap, needles, cloth. Mostly necessities. Sometimes a piece of leather, lace, a pretty ribbon.

Zisa heard the door open and close behind her in the twilight.

"Papa. Is that you?" she called.

An affirmative grunt greeted her ear. "Who else were you expecting?"

"No one, Papa. Ruchel will come tomorrow, maybe. Shall I make tea, Papa?"

"No. Sit. I will put up the water."

She heard the pot clatter as he put it on the stove. He opened the door of the stove to put more wood in. The fire had dropped low.

"Shall I help you start the fire again?"

"No, no. It's all right. Sit, child. Shall I rub your foot? Is the pain better?"

"Better, Papa."

She saw him rise against the outline of the black metal stove as the fire flickered up gaily. One hand swung loosely by his side, attached by a string of muscle and little else under the shirt it seemed. Dead for all purposes. The hand he had held up to protect his face, a hand no more. Ruchel could hold no hand up to protect herself. They were tied behind her back when they slashed her face. The lovely face now scarred with unseeing eyes. Nathan the bridegroom who could be no bridegroom to anyone after the attack. In the village there were only the dead and the maimed.

After Mama was found dead, Papa tried to drink. He tried because he had seen or heard of others. He could not drink. He would only get sick. He could only remember. With each swing and drop against his body, his dead arm would not let him forget.

Papa brought Ruchel to visit the next day. The girls sat and talked near the open window. Papa fixed tea and set the chess pieces on a table which he pushed toward the window.

Zisa took a seat opposite Ruchel and helped Papa set up the board. He pulled a chair up to the table for himself and called the moves for Ruchel as she played. He placed Ruchel's fingers on the piece she declared and reminded her of the previous move. The board imaged, Ruchel made her move. Papa set straight any pieces knocked down making the move. The wind fluttered the window's tattered curtain. Gradually night fell and they remembered they hadn't eaten yet. Ruchel's mother would be waiting for her, so Papa walked her home while Zisa fixed leftover vegetables for dinner. She trimmed the hardened crust from a small loaf of bread. Part of the crust she put in a drawer; some she threw out the window for the birds and small animals.

Zisa then cleared the chess board and pieces from the table and moved it slowly back to the center of the room. She lit the evening candle and set the table. Papa returned and they ate, finishing dinner with tea and a few cookies left from the sabbath meal. At dawn Papa would go to check the vegetable patch and water the young sprouts. The woodcutter who could no longer cut wood, the teamster who could no longer drive, Papa watered the garden and picked the weeds that would choke off the new plants. This was their crop for fall.

Zisa watched the flickering candle as it lit a circle in the small room. Within its warmth was life. Within its light was hope, hope deeply buried with the shoots under the earth waiting to come forth.

The Match

RABBI WILOFSKY sat in his study. For three years he had been trying to find a student to assist him—an apt, bright, ambitious boy with Talmudic leanings. He hadn't found him yet. Not that they hadn't presented themselves, but this one was too frivolous, this one stupid, or lazy in scholarly pursuits. Where would he find the right one? He would again write to Reb Gimmel in the nearby town for suggestions. Perhaps he knew of someone, and he would also write to the Rabbi of the big synagogue in Lvov, a Talmudic center which had a large Yeshiva. Surely one such as he had in mind could be found among all these Talmudic scholars.

They came. They went. None pleased Rabbi Wilofsky. Same shortcomings—too slow, too inept, too illiterate for his needs. He was not running a kindergarten for Talmudic students. He was accused of wanting a full fledged Baal Shem Tov by the Rabbis whose students he continued to reject.

Day after day he continued to clamor and complain about the lack of assistance in his growing synagogue, and day after day he interviewed and tried new young men. One day his daughter Leah stopped by and told him that she had heard of a young man newly arrived in Padorsk, a town nearby. Her cousin Rachel had written to her of a young man visiting his uncle in Padorsk. He had studied in Minsk and was on his way to Lvov to continue his studies. Her cousin, Leah said, thought he might be worth interviewing.

"What would she know?" interspersed the Rabbi, "and why didn't she write to me then, why you?"

"Obviously because you don't think she knows anything, as you just said. Shall I tell her to ask him to stop by on his way to Lvov?"

The Rabbi was noncommital.

"There's nothing to lose in just talking to him, is there? You can give him a short interview—just a few minutes. You already know what to look for."

The Rabbi coughed into his beard.

"All right. I'll see the young man. For just a few minutes. You're right—it won't hurt."

The letter was dashed off to her cousin. Leah watched for the young man to arrive by wagon in the next few days. He did. On Friday a cart stopped at the Rabbi's house. A young man with large hat, long coat and dark beard dismounted, brushed the hay from his coat and made his way to the Rabbi's door.

Leah opened the door for him and dropped her eyes as was proper for a young unmarried woman before a man, especially one bound for the rabbinate. She escorted him to her father's study after showing him where to store his bag of personal belongings.

She ushered him into the room and briskly departed down the hall, then tiptoed back to stand within earshot of the open door.

"You are from Proskorov, I have been told."

"Yes," said the young man. "My Rabbi wanted me to spend two years with the Rinanski Rabbis."

"Ha, they can teach you more than I can—here, read this passage for me, if you will, please."

The Rabbi opened a text on his desk and demonstrated the passage. The young man read, chanting the Hebrew in the required inflection, flowing the syllables from his tongue. The Hebraic passage sang.

Leah clenched her fingers into fists as she listened. Enchanting. Such perfection. The voices of the men mingled as they talked, the

Rabbi questioning, the young man answering straightforward staccato answers.

Their conversation relaxed slowly and flowed smoothly from monosyllables into sentences. When Leah brought in tea and prune cookies, the Rabbi was narrating an incident to illustrate a point of Kashruth that was under consideration. "An accidental drop of milk on the meat in a poor woman's house."

The young man was listening politely, attentively and interspersed his point with questions. The evening went. The tea went. The hours flew by and the Rabbi asked the young man to stay for dinner, as he was wont to do with his young interviewees, and to spend the night since this was already the Sabbath.

Leah ran up the stairs to help her mother prepare the guest room. Together they aired the room again, plumping a pillow, smoothing a spread, shaking curtains. They refreshed and retouched the room, with one eye on the Sabbath dinner cooking in the kitchen.

Leah's feelings toward the young man were evident to her mother. No need for words. Feyge Gittel was aware of the girl's heightened interest, her sharp glances and watchfulness, the fleeting daydreams in her eyes.

Arie Fidel stayed with them two days. It was time for him to continue his journey. Feyge watched her daughter's anxiety mount and she decided to throw her weight, whatever she could muster, in her daughter's direction—if only her husband were amenable.

She ran over to her neighbor, the widow Frau Momsel, and unburdened herself over a glass of tea. The widow was an interested, concerned listener, wise in these things. Thinking as she listened, when the Rabbi's wife finished, she asked, "Feyge Gittel, has the Rabbi ever really considered an assistant? Was there ever one who pleased him?"

"No, not really that I can remember. They all had failings."

"In scholarship?"

"Sometimes as students, sometimes personal habits or appearance—they were not serious enough. You never knew exactly what displeased him or why the young man fell short. Once he was interested in a young man whom he heard was favored by a Rabbi in Rovna, but he didn't read as well as his own students."

"Which Rabbi does your husband have a great respect for? More than ordinary?" asked Frau Momsel.

"He is very fond of Reb Levsky of Perdincheneff."

"He sees him frequently?"

"Every few months."

"Is there someone he reveres by reputation? Someone whose name carries weight?"

"Everyone has heard of Reb Gutchinev of Ploskoff."

"Right. Everyone has."

"So?" asked Feyge.

"What if he were known to have an interest or liking for this young man?"

"But Reb Gutchinev has never heard of him."

"How do you know?"

"What do you mean, how do I know?" asked Feyge.

"You have no way of knowing that he isn't interested in the young man," answered Frau Momsel.

"True...." Feyge Gittel sipped her tea, already cooled by their conversation.

"Some more hot tea, Feyge?" asked Momsel.

"No, no, I must run home and get the Rabbi's lunch. He's at the Talmud Torah with the students discussing one of the famous malameds."

"Run, then," Frau Momsel poured herself another glass of tea. "Remember Reb Gutchinev."

"Yes, yes, I'll remember...." Feyge stood, unhitched her dress from her waist and left.

Rabbi Wilofsky was already in the house when his wife came in. He was offering the young man a clean towel as he finished washing his hands.

The Rabbi seemed a little annoyed that his wife was not home when he came—that she had not anticipated his homecoming. But Leah had done the amenities, the washing of the hands.

Feyge Gittel was surprised to find her daughter had also prepared lunch—but then not surprised, considering the situation. The table was set not in the usual appointed linen of daily use. A Sabbath cloth, and a larger than usual bowl of wild flowers sat in the middle of the table. The extra adornments escaped the Rabbi who was busily discussing the merits of a particularly controversial dissertation recently ruled on by the orthodox synod.

"Rabbi Neuhafter is sometimes foolish, very like an old woman in his cautiousness. He skirts the issue trying to appease both sides and then no one is satisfied, but here he completely evaded the issue. Like an ostrich, he buried his head deeper in the old tractates and came up with such obscure, archaic resolutions that no one could accept. But there it was: Rabbi Heshel Ben Shlomo had ruled this was on such and such a day." He waved his hands in exasperation.

Mrs. Wilofsky slipped by the men back into the kitchen. Leah was puttering, looking for things to busy herself with, an excuse to stay close to the dining room.

The men's voices rose and fell in their discussion. The young man rising and responding to each dialectic thrust. They laughed frequently. Leah listened. She hugged her mother before she realized all that her enthusiasm told. Feyge smiled and hugged her back, giving the young cheek a kiss. They stood with their arms around each other's waists, listening—thinking.

That night as the Rabbi and Feyge Gittel retired, Feyge remarked on what a bright young man the newest visitor was. The Rabbi agreed.

"And so likeable, no?" she asked.

"I guess so."

He covered his head with the blanket. Feyge looked at her husband.

"I hear that Reb Gutchinev has a real liking for the boy."

"Where did you hear that?"

"Someone in the village mentioned it."

"Who is the someone?" he asked.

Feyge clutched her chest. The falsehood would strangle her.

"Oh—I hear so many things during the day," she said lightly. "Let's go to sleep."

"Yes, dear."

She slipped into her nightclothes. Unwilling to put down the thread of conversation, she addressed herself to the blanket.

"Leah seems to like this young man. . . ."

"Uh?"

"I must remember to get the down 'uberbet' ready for winter," she said thinking aloud as she looked at the blanket. "It's too warm for it yet, but it won't be long."

The blanket was quiet. Asleep?

"He is a nice young man, isn't he?"

"We agreed on that already. Go to sleep."

Soon it was morning. Feyge rushed to the kitchen to prepare breakfast. Arie had spoken of leaving that day since he was expected in Lvov that week. Her husband had already left for the synagogue with Arie for the early service. They would be back shortly for breakfast.

She wanted to speak to her husband before he left for the synagogue, but the men were so busy talking she could not manage to see him alone to discuss what had lain uppermost in her mind all night. Would he like the boy, this young man, in the synagogue and school with him and at home? He must realize that Leah was of marriageable age. He had performed the wedding ceremony for several of her friends this year.

Feyge managed to corner the Rabbi as he came into the house. Arie had gone to wash before breakfast. Feyge usually had little difficulty expressing herself to her husband. Finally grasping courage by the collar, desperately she thrust herself in front of her husband.

"Yacov, I must talk to you—it can't wait!"

"Oh—not even till after breakfast?"

"No, I must talk to you now."

"All right. You seem troubled. Did Mrs. Feingold find fault with your honey-cake like last year?"

"No, nothing like that. It's about Leah."

"Yes. What about Leah?"

"Leah is going to be eighteen this June."

"Yes."

"Don't you think we should look for a husband for her?"

He looked hard at her, "Are you worried about her being a spinster already?"

"No, of course not."

"So?"

"Yacov...." She bit her lip, hesitating to finish the thought.

"Yes?"

"Yacov, do you think you'll ever find an assistant you will approve of one hundred percent?"

"I should hope. What has that to do with Leah?"

"I think she rather likes Arie."

He looked at her. Stroked his beard meditatively.

"That might present a problem," he said.

She looked surprised.

"What if he's spoken for?"

She gasped, "I hadn't thought of that. How foolish of me. Oh, my poor child." She began to cry.

"No, no. It's all right. I wanted to make sure of things before I spoke. He is free and very willing to be my assistant—and my son-in-law." Feyge smiled through her tears, and dabbed them away with her apron.

"The letter has already gone to Lvov and to his father. Tell your daughter that if Reb Gutchinev thinks so highly of this young man, why shouldn't I?" He winked in the direction of the kitchen. "Come let's eat."

Out of Egypt

EVERY FRIDAY night Yentel would invite Hershel Loshik to share her Sabbath meal and every Friday night he refused. Since he was one of the few eligible bachelors in the village, Yentel couldn't, wouldn't give up, but she had to find outside help in getting Hershel into her home. How would she show him what a fine cook and housekeeper she was? And it was hard for him to refuse her after a hard day on the road, grinding scissors, running odd errands, hard to refuse a good meal at a clean table. But Hershel was afraid.

His mother had been a shrew, so he had been told. He himself had never known her. She had run off with a tailor who later deserted her and she pined away at her parents' home. Hershel's father had brought him and his sister Fanya up. Brought up? That is fed and clothed until ten and then apprenticed. Fanya had become a cook's helper and Hershel a wheedler of knives, needles, scissors and farming tools. More than this he didn't know. He would sneak into cheder to sit and listen with the other students. When they saw the boy's interest, the Rabbi and teachers helped him. In this way he learned to read and write a little. Enough to keep accounts if not to study. Later he was sent to join a group of orphans to study for bar mitzvah, and learned enough to handle the service which demanded that he be called up to Torah on a Sabbath morning.

After this was accomplished he rarely attended services. Only the high holidays and special occasions induced him into the synagogue.

He was married under the canopy at twenty to a pretty young girl—a match arranged between his master and the bride's father. Shortly after the ceremony, she drove him from the house.

"A scissor grinder! Is that all you want to be? That any idiot can do. Why not a store, a small shop to begin with? Even a tailor or shoemaker would be better!"

Her ambition drove him from the house into the tavern. What else was open to an oppressed Jew when all his brethren were preparing for the daily evening meal or the Sabbath? One could not intrude on neighbors every night. The tavern was warm, friendly and undiscriminating. He met other marital outcasts there—peasants, officers, scholars. They toasted each other with beer, wine, or vodka, and talked philosophy until the stars became transparent in the sky and it was safe to go home to sleep. The women had given up.

When his wife died in childbirth a few years later, Hershel made his home his headquarters again. He left the tavern and only occasionally had cronies in for beer and cards. He enjoyed the peaceful stillness of the house and began to read again.

Yentel tried. Finally she went to the Rabbi. The matchmaker offered her no hope or solace. Hershel was not approachable. But when the Rabbi spoke to him and said it would be a mitzvah to share a Sabbath meal with a lonely soul and besides what was there for him to be afraid of, Hershel said maybe he would sometime. He was not going to be snagged by Sabbath candles and holiday linen or trapped by the smell of hot freshly baked challah and gefullte fish. And the thought of a woman in bed—there was too much heartache, too many problems to hurdle and atone for that pleasure.

She asked and he answered. Always in the negative. He was busy with other friends or too tired. Sabbaths ran by. Holidays came—a short one, a long one. Soon it was Passover. Yentel had been asked to Yonia's, widow Ruchel's son's, seder, out of kindness of their hearts and the need to fulfill the commandment to house a stranger that evening. She accepted and mentioned Hershel, since she told the widow Ruchel that she had intended to ask him to help her make her seder.

The widow Ruchel, a wise old woman, not too old to have forgotten her own early romantic dreams, chuckled over this and insisted upon inviting Hershel also to her son's seder. There would be many children, Yonia's in-laws and an uncle from a nearby town. Another addition would hardly be noticed. They were already planning to stand the bed against the wall in one room to enable the table to run the length of the house—that is, through the living room and kitchen—and opening the bedroom alcove gave them room for at least seven or eight more.

For two months now, Ruchel had been fattening three geese for this occasion. The fish she was expecting momentarily, and the matzohs had already been checked by the Rabbi. It would be a wonderful seder. The wine-merchant Max had set aside a gallon of wine. Ruchel was running home to prepare the Passover dishes, to empty cupboards, clean the crumbs with the prescribed ritual feather, and burn the chumitz. The very air was festive.

Elijah would be coming to help them celebrate and enjoy Moses' leaving Egypt—leading his people out of bondage. A wonderful holiday. The children had been coached in the four questions to be asked every Passover by the youngest in each family. Ruchel went on and on, bubbling, as she ran home from the market.

Yentel was pleased too. Hershel would probably accept Ruchel's invitation to the seder. After all, there was no danger in that and she hoped that Ruchel wouldn't mention that she, Yentel, would be there. That might prejudice him. Surprised as guest-strangers was a much easier role.

It was a wonderful seder. The children had new clothes. Everyone wore his party best. Hershel was seated with the other men on pillow-padded chairs. All assembled around the table with chairs squeezed together so tightly only those strategically assigned to serve the food could move out of their seats. They laughed when elbows clashed as they reached into their plates and bowls.

"Hey, that's my plate you're eating from!" yelled little Shimme at his sister. "That's yours there!"

"Children. Let's be quiet. The Zaydee is reading. Follow in your Haggadahs," said Ruchel.

What a seder. The dishes clicked against each other as they touched on the table. The mounded platters clanked their weight against the table as they were set down. So many plates and platters filled the table; the clean white tablecloth barely showing between them occasionally made room for a little wine spill as an elbow was jostled.

First came the fish; juicy soft gefullte fish with cooked carrots on the side and horseradish. Next came the soup, steaming hot chicken broth floating round light tender matzoh balls. The salt and pepper passed back and forth.

Then came Ruchel's pièce de resistance: the baked geese, stuffed. The aroma of the steaming brown birds filled the room. The smell alone melted in the mouth and created hunger anew. Stuffed kishka and potato kugel accompanied the geese.

Time moved the plates, emptied them and replaced them with others. The dessert was readied to join the hot tea as it was served.

So they celebrated the Exodus from Egypt. They celebrated all the going outs, the leavings and enterings of many lands through so many years; finishing the endless seder courses, explaining meanings anew with bantering questions and solutions. The prescribed four glasses drunk, the ten plagues honored, counted and recounted in the text in ordered sequence early in the meal, the Hillel sandwich, the moror and charoses, the bitter herbs and mortar and finally the opening of the door for Elijah.

The children screamed. They watched Elijah's glass to see if the wine diminished, and to make sure the adults were not shaking the table. Elijah came and went. The company sang Passover songs finally coming to the hagadyoh, the ditty of the one more kid. Passover. The final benediction, the prayer "and next year in Jerusalem" with a tear. The ending of the beautiful seder.

The women kissed each other goodnight, and somehow Yentel found Hershel walking her home. After all he couldn't refuse Ruchel's request and let Yentel walk the streets alone so late. They walked in silence, warmed by the four glasses of wine and the hot tea and kuchen.

Yentel wanted to make conversation but was afraid to. She might so easily say the wrong thing. Hershel was so sensitive. Who knew how he would take any comment of hers?

She wanted to ask him how his business was, but that might be interpreted as prying. If she asked to borrow one of his books she knew he liked to read he might feel she was getting too personal. So they walked in silence. Not a word passed between them under the moon. If she could have tripped or known how to trip, Yentel would have fallen straight to earth. Anything to elicit a response from this young, strong, silent, stubborn man. And so they walked to her house, with only the sounds of their footsteps on the ground.

They said goodnight at her door. She bit her lip after he left. She had rehearsed so many clever things to say. So many pertinent, unobtrusive comments hoarded away for just such an occasion.

She tripped on the rung of a chair as she groped in the dark for the candles, and giggled in exasperation until tears flowed. Then she began to laugh at herself. No more nonsense. This coy girl role was not for her. She went to sleep, plotting. Discarding and sifting some of the plans. To show interest and not be too anxious. To show that she was ambitious for him and yet not appear pushy. How not to appear too cold and yet not too warm. She covered herself with these thoughts and fell asleep.

The morning sun foretold a very warm day. Yentel got up quickly before it got too hot. She dressed and tidied up and thought of taking a book down to the spring after she picked up the chicken that she had left in Frieda Schochat's cool cellar on the way home from the market yesterday. She tied a bright kerchief around her neck and combed her hair with extra care. Hershel might just have not left town yet, unlikely as that seemed.

And there he was, walking through the streets talking with Chaim Bentoff. When she noticed that he saw her, she smiled quickly at him and directed her feet on their planned course to Frieda's, hastening the pace just a little not to appear to saunter as if waiting for him to catch up with her.

Yesterday at this time, she had seen him talking to vendors and buying eggs at the market. She had stopped at the fish stall to look at the pike swimming in the tub, hoping he would notice her. She lingered, watching the fish. No, that wasn't what she wanted for lunch, but she bought some to justify her standing there so long.

At Frieda's Yentel was offered tea even before Frieda went down into the cellar to retrieve Yentel's chicken. Yentel had to accept.

"All right. I'll have a quick sip," she said to Frieda's insistent offer.

The chicken, brought up from the cellar, was placed on a small table near the stove while Frieda fixed their tea.

"A little kugel to go with the tea?" Frieda pressed.

"No. No, thank you. I have been eating too much already this Passover, and it only began last night," She sipped the hot tea. It was too hot to sip fast.

"Frieda, do you still have the book your uncle sent you from Odessa? The one with Bialik's newest poems?" she asked.

"Yes."

"May I borrow it for a day or two?"

"Of course."

Yentel finished her tea. "I must be going—I still have a few things to prepare for tonight."

"You're having a seder?"

Yentel nodded.

"Many guests?"

"No. Just myself."

"Come eat with us tonight. I had no idea."

"Thank you, Frieda, but I know how crowded you are already. I don't know where you'll put them all." Her eyes swept from the tiny kitchen to the small antechamber which served as a dining room. How had they managed last night?

"One more won't matter anymore, I don't think," said Frieda.

"No, no. I really couldn't," Yentel bowed out, "Thank you for the book. I'll take good care of it."

Having forgotten to bring her basket, Yentel tucked the chicken under an arm. As she walked, the repossessed chicken swung its neck from under one arm; under the other Bialik nestled. She felt the small plump hen against her. She had gotten to the market early that day, when the selection was still good. Cleanly dressed with a little smoldering of the pin feathers, it would be ready for the pot. Yentel marched home. Yentel, chicken, Bialik.

Going up the street back to her house, she passed Fanya Gittel's open door and paused to toss her head through the doorway for a quick holiday greeting. Coming in her direction a few feet away was Hershel. She continued her walk. As she passed him she smiled.

"You're still in town this morning?" she asked.

He stopped to answer.

"Yes. I had almost forgotten and thanks to the Rabbi's reminding me yesterday that today is my mother's yahrzeit. Pessye Cohen is taking me in for the second seder, so I will spend the holidays here after all." Everyone knew about Hershel's offhand observance of the holidays. He was hard pressed to stop work for the Sabbath at times. The Rabbi, it was told, worried that he was drifting away.

Yentel pointed to the chicken under her arm.

"She and I will share my seder tonight. But while she is cooking I'll go down to the brook with Bialik."

"Bialik?"

"The poet." She lifted the book for him to see. "My uncle in Odessa sent me this book of his poems."

"My uncle," she had said! Why? Why was she running on like this? It was no crime to be alone in the world, though she would love to have claimed a living relative somewhere.

"I lent it to Frieda," she continued clutching book and chicken, "and picked it up with my chicken that she so kindly put into her

cooling cellar. We're running into such unseasonably hot weather—
and the brook is the only spot that doesn't roast when it gets so
hot. So while the chicken is cooking I'll go sit near the brook and
read if there's time under one of the large shady trees. So I must
hurry and start things before it gets too hot to cook. Good day,
Hershel, and a good holiday to you." She smiled and walked the
chicken off with a cavalier clip, the head and neck swinging against
her skirt behind her.

Soon she had everything in the kitchen in order prepared for the
seder. The chicken soup simmered. The lamb bone, the burnt egg,
all the symbolic ingredients required by the Passover ritual service
were being put into place.

She put a Haggadah on the table near the candles. It was
strange. Unusual. Table set for one. Well, not really just one. She
took her father's large glass from the cupboard. Large and special.
Yentel washed it until it sparkled and dried it carefully. Elijah's cup.
That she set on a small tray in the center of the table. Elijah visited
everyone this night. She set a small bottle of holiday wine next to
the glass.

She would be alone, but not lonely. Tonight a Jew was not lonely
anywhere—he belonged to the thousands, millions everywhere
observing the seder. He belonged to the countless numbers who
had observed the celebration of the Exodus from almost the year
following their deliverance from Egypt.

She sighed. It would have been nice to have had others at the
table. But she could also have gone to Frieda's if she had
preferred—no, this was better. She put the matzohs, the required
three, in their place on the seder table.

There was only a short time left before sunset. The day had run
by and Yentel had not had the leisure to take Bialik to the brook.
She quickly finished tidying up. Why am I working like a horse, she
asked herself as she swept behind doors and chased cobwebs from
corners. For whom am I cleaning? It must be for Elijah. It's an old
habit from my mother. For a holiday everything must be in its
place, spotless and shining.

The soup tasted ready. The chicken was tender. She would have to do without fish, she decided as she smelled the fish she had cooked the day before. It had been too warm today. On well, there would be more than enough to eat. She had fixed a small potato kugel. Hard boiled eggs and salt water and the necessary greens were all set out.

As dusk gathered outside, she took off her apron and hung it on a kitchen chair. She combed her hair and washed up. Slowly she brought the steaming soup to the table. The chicken queened a platter. Carrots were ladled onto a small plate.

She sat down at the table, opened the Haggadah and read:

> Welcome to the Seder! Tonight we observe a most ancient, colorful, and significant festival. The Seder takes us back to those events which occurred more than three thousand years ago. We recall the Egyptian bondage of the Children of Israel, and their deliverance by God. . . . We begin this service by sanctifying the name of God and proclaiming the holiness of this Festival. . . .

Suddenly there was a knock on the door. Who? Too early for Elijah. What nonsense! Elijah didn't have to knock. Doors were opened for him.

Yentel opened the door. There on the step stood Hershel. She was stunned.

"Is something wrong?' she asked quickly. "Have you come for me? Is someone ill?"

"No. . . no." He smiled. "I met the widow Ruchel today and she said you. . . ." He hesitated trying to find the words with his mouth, ". . . you wouldn't be at their seder tonight."

"Yes," she nodded. "They had asked me, but I felt I couldn't impose on them again for another seder, and Frieda asked too. But you. . . ." She stopped and thought, puzzled ". . . you were going to Pessye's?"

"That's true. And I did go there. I thought. . . well, when we began reading the Haggadah about strangers being taken in this night. The mitzvah of the act, and I realized..." He plowed into the rest of the sentence with one breath, "...that you would be alone, tonight of all nights when it is prescribed by law..."

"By law?"

"Well, it says in the..."

She agreed.

"And anyhow," he continued, "since I am in need of a mitzvah, I felt by coming to your seder tonight I would serve *two*."

"Two?"

"Yes. One: you would not be alone, which is technically forbidden tonight. And two: I would be the stranger you are commanded to take in this night. Just as it is written in the Haggadah."

She laughed.

"I see you have the text open already." He nodded toward the table.

"I had just begun to read. Here, let me take your coat."

He wouldn't relinquish it and draped it over a chair.

"Can I do something?" he asked.

"No, no. I have everything ready. Just another fork and knife, if you would be so kind."

He set them on the table next to the plate she was placing opposite hers. She filled the newly added wineglass.

"Please sit down," she said.

He did.

She looked at him and smiled, "Now you will have to do the honor of leading the service. It is prescribed that way, no?"

He opened his Haggadah and began the first passage. She trembled. Her joy trembled inside of her. Suddenly she was afraid. Afraid to look at him. He read in a strong voice, sure and clear.

He stopped and she looked up hoping that he would not see the tears gathering in her eyes. He was smiling at her.

"Yentel, drink your wine. It's time now." He patted the Haggadah. "And refill the glasses. We've got a long way to go before we get out of Egypt tonight."

Nissun's Dawn

Nissun walked slowly, looking at the sky, watching the clouds moving over the earth; silent, dark, they fled toward the horizon covering the earth's rotating bulk with hazy gray movement.

He walked the back way through open dead fields looking at the sky as the withered winter ground stretched before him. His frozen fingers twisted around the book in his pocket. The family would still be asleep when he arrived and he would have time to rest a while before they moved into the kitchen with the early morning rush.

Motya would greet him and try to sit next to him during breakfast, his little face watching Nissun's every move. How was his trip? Did he find a job? Was there a possibility of his going to school? Could they visit him at Uncle Avrum's?

He had time to answer these questions. He unlocked the door and let himself into the house quietly, hoping the door would not give him away. It squeaked gently, tiredly, as he closed it. The light was coming through the windows, seeping by the slits on the side and center partings of the curtains. It was much lighter outside in the near dawn.

Nissun took a candle from a drawer and set it in the candlestick on the table, struck a match and lit it. There in the narrow light of the candle he removed his coat and cap and lay them across the seat of a wooden kitchen chair. He moved slowly, afraid that the squeak of his shoes or his weight on a loose board would tell his mother he was home. There was still time before the family woke for breakfast. He felt the kettle on the stove. Still hot. The wood burning in the stove had kept the water hot. He poured some into a glass, added a few drops of soaking concentrated tea from the cracked teapot and sat down at the table.

His book was in his coat pocket. Briefly he considered getting up for it but sat gorged with the peace of this quiet moment. The tea tasted good after the morning cold. It would soon be summer—the last frost had passed. Spring would be pushing its way through the dormant earth before long and trees would begin to bud little knobs of green which would open to pink and white blossoms.

He started. Was someone getting up? He hoped not—not yet. He wanted to sit a little longer by himself.

Poor Mama, so hopeful that her brother would be able to take him in at least for a year or two. She didn't know that Uncle Avrum had been ill and that Yonkel, his oldest son, not too much older than Nissun himself, was running the farm. Perhaps, they had told him if the summer was very good, he could come in the fall and help them with the harvest.

Pachefka was a large town. It had three schools and its own hospital. Much larger than any city he had ever seen. Nissun sipped his hot tea slowly. His fingers warmed, relaxing around the glass. He was not unhappy to be home again. Soon Mama would waken, come in, kiss him and fix him a special breakfast. Six months would go quickly enough. The birds were beginning to waken outside. Their chirps came through the window with the brightening rays of light.

Yes, soon Mama would waken. When she saw him, he could hear her say, as she put her arms around him, "What a long walk you've had. How tired you must be, my little man. Sit and I will fix you something hot to eat while you tell me all that happened."

And later when he told her the news, she'd say "Oh, it will wait then. We will be the lucky ones to have you here for a few months more."

Nissun sat dreaming to himself, lapping up the quiet moments. Suddenly as he dozed he heard a rustling. The door opened behind him and slammed.

"You're back?"

He turned sideways in his chair and glanced up at his mother as she strode by him to the stove, her dark shawl tightly drawn to her. Her brows knit as she felt the outside of the kettle. She mumbled something he did not catch and turned to pick up a glass.

"You're back!" She appraised him. "So they didn't want you either. And we'll still have your big mouth to feed until something else is worked out."

She poured herself a glass of tea and sat down opposite him at the table. "I knew it! There are no favors from brothers. Only your father is foolish enough to believe that he would help. A dreamer."

Her uncombed hair fell into her face. She got up and rattled a drawer looking for a spoon. Muttering to herself she drew apart the curtains of the window before she sat down. The sun plunged past the shabby curtains and threw its beams across the room. Cold light swept the spring back and winter sat in his stomach.

In The Time Of The Russias

IN THE TIME of the Russias, of the heavy czars, a mountain stood near the village of Blettel. The mountain, little larger than a hill, stood over the small houses that clustered close to its base. The wheat fields lay on either side of the village, a forest in the distance.

Life seemed good, peaceful, quiet. The chickens clucked their strutting steps, head in air, breasts out, pleased with themselves and their pecking. The cows lowed in the meadows, lazing in the sun, chewing leisurely and moving home at sunset. Goats scampered tossing their beards, suspicious of the sheep that shared their fence, their stalls.

Mechel looked at the sheep in his farmyard—gentle, stupid animals, good only for wool and eating, he thought. Many a night he had had to get up with an ax or gun to chase away a fox or wolf when he heard their frantic baas. Too often the kill had been executed—a torn lamb remained or was made off with, while the others huddled together at the barn door or gateposts. As often as he'd pit his wits against the marauders, as often he lost. The wolves would leap the fence, or burrow through a patched hole in the barn gate. The rams were as helpless as the lambs, their large horns of no avail. They didn't know how to use them.

Minka, the milk cow, looked at him with sad, large eyes as he approached. He stroked the ram's back. "Much good we did when we domesticated you. Now you are helpless and those out there..." He pointed to the dark outdoors, "...are getting smarter every day. Better you had remained wild and ruthless, if ever you were." He scratched his head with fingers protruding from torn gloves.

"Each winter I lose four or five of you. Almost a sacrifice to a winter god," he whispered to himself. He stroked the ram's head. "Poor innocent. Eh, I have to find some better way to protect you."

He locked the barn door behind him, bolting it with a heavy crossbar. Returned to the house in the dark. In the distance the light crept over the mountain. There was not much time left for sleep tonight.

Mechel removed his hastily put on boots and set them near the bed. Bayle, his wife, slept on. She had not heard the commotion from the barnyard. Luckily he had, else they could have lost all the animals. One never knew in dry weather whether it was a single animal or raiding pack.

Toward dawn Mechel heard horses approaching. A dream he thought. Then he sat up and listened. As he put on his boots, the door burst open. Four Cossacks entered with sabers drawn. Bayle sat up in bed and began to whimper when she saw them. Mechel, unaware of what he did, stroked her through the blanket with his eyes on the soldiers. "Quiet, heart...."

The soldiers approached the bed.

"Get it over, Pesekoff. Then we'll eat," one of them said.

"Wait," the one addressed answered. He sheathed his saber.

"Let them feed us."

"Yes, my lords, let me get you some bread and cheese."

"No meat?" one of the Cossacks asked.

"We have none—not prepared," Mechel answered.

"You have sheep, goats, cows."

Mechel nodded vigorously. "Yes, a few but...they have to be slaughtered and prepared...even a chicken needs a little time."

The other Cossacks leaned on their sabers, smiling.

"Show us the animals, Mr. Farmer," Pesekoff said.

"Of course." Mechel put his other boot on and got up from the bed. Bayle cowered in the pillows.

"She can stay here," one of the Cossacks said when Bayle attempted to get out of bed and follow him.

Mechel led the way to the barn. Unbolted the door. Daylight seeped in with them as they entered. The two goats were asleep in their stall, nestled against each other. The ram, the dam and ewes sat up on the straw as the visitors approached. Minka blinked. Natasha the mare stood by herself in a corner unwilling to be awakened yet. Perhaps pretending to be asleep and not ready for mowing or taking the cart to the village.

Pesekoff approached the animals and looked at Mechel.

"Vladimir," he said to one of his fellows, "I hear that Jews are very humane and slaughter their animals without pain." Vladimir laughed.

"Shall we ask him for a demonstration?"

"Yes, Jew farmer," Pesekoff spat on the ground. "Show us how you slaughter painlessly."

"Do you want a lamb or a ewe, sir?"

"Either will do."

Mechel reached for the slaughterer's knife that he kept sharpened carefully and ran his finger across the blade to make sure there was no nick in the metal that might cause pain to the animal. The cut had to be straight and clean across the jugular to offer the least pain and the easiest death to the animal. He looked at the sheep, the ram standing there amidst the ewes and lambs, huddled together from the cold.

"If you don't hurry we'll do it for you," said one of the Cossacks, reaching for the saber at his belt. The others brandished theirs in chopping motions. "It might not be as painless."

Mechel approached a little lamb and attempted to lead it away. It began to baa and he lifted it in his arms.

"Where are you taking it?" asked Pesekoff. "Get it over with, now."

"In front of the ram and its ewe? Surely I can take it outside—I'll be quick."

"No. Now."

Mechel set the lamb down and held its head next to his knee, lifted the little head to bare the throat, and with a quick stroke slit. The lamb fell to its side as blood gushed from the cut, and thrashed as the blood seeped into the straw. The smell of the blood leaped to his nostrils as Mechel stood up. The other animals were beginning to panic. He stroked the ram and the ewe.

"Continue," said Pesekoff.

"Sir?"

"The ram next. . . we need lots of meat to take with us."

Mechel approached the ram and slew him. The dam next as they requested, the goats, and they ordered the cow.

"But sirs, how will you carry all this?" Mechel asked.

"Don't worry. We may borrow your cart."

Covered with blood, Mechel approached Minka. He could not make her kneel and had to deliver the stroke from underneath. She stood for a long time dripping blood and he had to cut her again. She stood mooing for a long time until she went down on her knees and lay with her eyes open.

"What about the horse?" asked one of the Cossacks. "He's just getting into practice—see how he wields his knife—a regular Cossack he could be."

"But the horse," Mechel stammered, "you could use it for the cart."

"We have our own," said Pesekoff.

"But sirs, the horse is not for eating! Why kill—why destroy it?"

"We don't eat Jews either," said Vladimir, sitting on a stack of hay. "So hurry it up."

Mechel killed the horse and staggered out of the barn. At saber point he was walked back to the house. The Cossacks opened the door and pushed him through.

"Finish the job, Jew. You're giving us lessons."

The sun came up full, shining over the mountains.

Schmiel Pinhas

SCHMIEL PINHAS brought his horse into the stall, gave it some hay, covered it with a torn burlap pad, and patted it good night. Good, faithful Manya—stalwart and steady, dependable, demanding little, never nagging. If wives only had such virtues. He scratched his head through his thick woolen hat with blue-cold fingers. The frost hung on the trees and clung on the ground, making the earth stone hard. Where does such painful cold come from? The black sky didn't answer. The light from his small hut stood yellow in the dark. It showed through the two small uneven windows, and through cracks in the walls.

He opened the door. Marusha was standing near the stove, sullenly stirring a boiling pot. She slammed the lid on it when she heard him enter the room. She walked into the curtained-off corner of the one-room hovel where their bed stood, without looking at him. Still angry he thought. She should cool off in a few hours. He threw his stiff heavy overcoat on a bench near the door and unwrapped the scarf from around his neck. He shoved his peddler's pack in a corner of the room near the door. It would have a day of rest tomorrow. The cold made it useless to try to travel the twenty miles to Odessa to sell the raisins and almonds his brother sent and usually kept him supplied with from the south.

Only then did a movement near the foot of the stove catch his eye. Little Masha was sitting there on a blanket, playing with a big wooden spoon. Her too short limp back was held upright with straps and strips of cloth against the back of the small chair she was seated in—a child's crude chair from which the legs had been removed—and her own legs jutted over the edge of the seat and lay flat on the earthen floor, one leg plump in its child's hightop shoe and the other shriveled and shorter, padded in the foot to fill the shoe. Masha looked up at him as she swung the spoon through the air and laughed alone in her happy little world. A summer smile from a happy glowing turnip face with gleaming eyes, which could only reflect, as she looked at him, the life from the flickering fire flaming through the grill of the stove.

Marusha was quiet behind the curtain. Perhaps asleep. Pinhas took a bowl which stood on a heavy oak table near the stove and began to fill it with the potato soup that was still simmering in the pot on the stove. He stirred the soup, trying to dislodge a piece of meat that might have fallen to the bottom of the pot as he spooned it into his not-too-clean bowl. He moved a rickety three-legged stool from under the table closer to the stove and seated himself on the stool, holding the bowl in one hand as he ate. He watched the child making silent noises with her mouth. Occasionally the spoon hit the ground but she never tired of waving it. He finished the soup and leaned over to put the bowl back on the table. He got up and with two steps glanced behind the curtain which didn't reach all the way to the wall. Marusha was still. He listened to her breathing. She was sleeping, lying crosswise on the bed with her thick boots on.

He turned back to the child, bent down and untied her from the chair frame, and lifted her into the air.

"Have you been a good girl?" he asked, and answered himself, "And how is she to be anything else?"

He sat down on the floor in front of the stove, on the dark earthen floor warmed by the heat of the wood stove. He held the child on his lap and patted her head, the spoon still waving, clenched in her rigidly held hand. She struck him once with it and he took it from her. No protest. The hand kept its fingers clenched. The arm still waved. Her gaze was on the stove, on the flames as they leaped and broke. It was warm and peaceful.

For the first time in a long while Pinhas thought of reading. He rose with the baby and looked into a corner where some books had once been piled. He had been a great reader in his student days. A candle or lantern was needed to see the titles, but he could bring them nearer the stove. They felt damp as he lifted two of them from the pile with one hand, holding Masha under his other arm. He'd better put the baby to bed first. Let the books remain for a minute; he'd be back for them.

He walked with the child into the corner behind the curtain and in the semi-dark of that curtained-off area put the little girl into the crib that stood next to the bed; settling her carefully and quietly, not to awaken Marusha. Let her anger sleep. Even in bed now he kept his distance, except for those intermittent moments when her wants needed fulfilling.

He tiptoed back to the pile of books and lifted several. He'd almost forgotten which ones he had there. He put them next to the stool and lit a large lantern. He sat on the stool and lifted one of the books; leaning toward the light, he opened the book, holding it in one hand he let it fall open in his hand. The smell of the paper pages rose to his nostrils. He turned to the title page—the binding was loose and pages began to come out as he turned them— MICHAEL STROGOFF. Great adventure, the freedom of the plains. His back was cramped. He lay down on the ground on his stomach, stretching himself full length in front of the stove. The lantern flickered but the light was adequate. He could make the words out. The cover of the book had some fungus mold on the corners, and the glue reeked, the smell clinging to his fingers. The yellowed pages were flaking as he turned them by their corners.

CHAPTER I. As he opened to the indicated page a tiny green curled worm uncurled itself and lifted its head.

"Well, little friend, do you mind if I dislodge you or may I at least share your pleasure? All right I won't evict you. You're little enough to work around. Besides let us enjoy the book and relish the sweetness of this silent, peaceful moment, and read together, shall we?" The worm stretched its tiny slightly opaque green body full length in the crevice of the page binding and slipped itself down into the binding.

Pinhas began to read. It was a rare night. Years ago—it seemed like years ago when they were first together and lived in Vilna, in a neat little house with curtains and a carriage stall—he could read in his study. So many candles were burned! Those were the good days. A warm house, linen to spare, veal and lamb and fresh eggs from the market. Now this barren farm. He was saving. Little by little perhaps someday they could go back.

He looked up from the book. The wind was whistling across the plain. A bitter cold night was ahead. He tried to keep his mind on the story that he had read so many years ago, but his mind would not leave its old memories. Marusha was the young wife of a doctor when he first saw her when he was a student in Moscow. He was pleased with what he saw and in the company of his friends was bold enough to show that to her. She blushed as she finished making her purchases in the market that morning. It was a lovely spring day and when her hat flew off her head, teased by a warm wind, he was the first to sprint after it and retrieve it. She thanked him quickly with an embarrassed smile as he handed it to her and left.

There had been other meetings after that, at first by chance and then no longer left to chance. He understood her. She loved him. And they wanted each other. And then she found herself pregnant. She could have stayed. Her husband was older but not that old, but she wanted them to bring up this child, and she could no longer tolerate her husband's carresses even if Pinhas could be magnanimous. She urged him to leave school, collect the money his family had provided for his education and maintenance until he could settle in some profession, and take her away from the tormenting existence she endured. He did. He had to after she came to him in the middle of the night.

He collected his funds and they left town. They found a lovely little house in Vilna, and lived there happily waiting for the baby to be born. And in due months the child was born—feeble, deformed, and with no evidence of any future intelligence as its early months moved by. (It was against God to wish these things, yet how could one not wish it? Still? He sighed.) City after city they canvassed for specialists in childhood diseases; they were disappointed by some and taken in by others. The money that was to have seen him through four or five years went, bit by bit. They borrowed heavily from their families, who couldn't bear to let them starve. Pinhas's older brother even set him up in a little business in a promising young town where a new railroad was being built. It was a good little store. It prospered for a while and things looked promising, but it needed more than one to run it. Marusha was too tired, too upset, too involved with the baby, who needed her all the time. They had to close the store. Other business ventures failed.

"Good evening little friend, are you coming back to check on my reading or my intelligence? I'm getting along just fine." The worm peered up from the binding at the edge of the book and crept back inside.

Yes, once he could almost read in peace sometimes. Before his reading made Marusha angry, before she blamed him for all their misfortunes. It became all his fault: the baby, the business failures. It was his passions she blamed; after all, it is always men leading to the downfall of women. Passions, he snickered; one has to have energy for passions. The night wore on and he enjoyed the quiet solitude of his thoughts. He wasn't too old yet. There was hope. There is always hope. Where there's life, there's hope, as the saying goes.

He suddenly heard Marusha stir and scramble to her feet. She yelled, "Pinhas, come quick! Something is wrong with the baby."

He ran to her and pulled the curtain back to let light into the crib. The baby was writhing and gurgling. Marusha lifted her up and put her on the bed. She began to gasp and turn blue.

"Quick, get the doctor from the village!" she screamed. She turned the child on its side and began to pat her hard on the back. He grabbed his overcoat and ran for the barn, hitched up the horse with cold trembling fingers and started for the village. Through the window he could see Marusha walking the floor furiously with the child in her arms.

The cold, dark silence struck at him as he drove the horse with panic. The wheels squealed on their wooden axles as the cart rumbled after the galloping hoofs of the horse. He urged the horse on. Suddenly the wheel of the cart struck a rock, the cart bounced, the horse to regain its balance jerked on the harness which snapped in the cold and the horse ran blindly, wildly ahead into the dark. Pinhas ran after it, calling the horse, but Manya had disappeared; even the sound of her clattering hoofs was gone. He ran on, changing his pace to a trot, hoping that some rider or some living creature would appear. He proceeded in the direction of the village. The night gathered around him and the cold rang in his ears.

He held his hands against his chest inside his coat. He walked for hours and as the sky lightened he sat down. The cold cut his breath. It came in short gasps of white vapor puffed into the blue air. He took his mittens off to rub his hands and rested one hand on the ground. He looked across the treeless plain for a bush or tree. He was still far from the village. He knew what the cold could do.

He looked at his hand as it lay on the ground, propping his weight on it before getting up. It was so blue and had begun sticking to the icy ground. He tried to move his fingers but he couldn't will them to contract; the muscles wouldn't twitch. He would have to harness all his strength to make the effort to get up. The ground was not releasing its hold. He no longer felt the cold, nor did his chest ache as he breathed. It was so quiet. A dead silence hung over the plain. Not a bird or insect moved. When he was found the next morning he was frozen to the cold ground.

Lemish's Wife

LEMISH WAS SWEET and gentle, large and rotund, and even when he growled, it was a big pussycat roar, which under even inexperienced handling, tapered to a purr.

His wife was a sore on the environment. Short and gray, she hobbled about on a gnarled cane with which she poked or fished rags out of shallow ponds and street ditches. She was looking for treasures. Anything anyone dropped or lost was her finding, her luck, her fortune; and all of these findings she scavenged, nested in a torn pillowcase under her bed. One day it might be a broken earring, a stocking with two holes, half a comb, a shoe without a heel, a heel without a shoe. There was no end to her findings.

Lemish knew of his wife's preoccupation, but who did it hurt? So he let things go, never criticizing or commenting on her habit. Meeme Ruchel, as she was called, never realized that she was bizarre in her nature, that human scavengers are rare. Not until the Edelfishes came into town.

A moderate, comfortably conforming family, they traveled from Vitebsk and roomed with Melosh the schochat, a distant relative not seen for many years. Mr. Edelfish was looking for a new business; if not new, an old one he could pick up. Something profitable and not too demanding of his time, since most of his time was spent watching Mrs. Edelfish and their two daughters. He loved them all dearly but they needed watching. Each had a wandering eye, and what they saw and liked, they followed. The girls had been in this habit as babies, and their mother had not broken them of it. And to make matters worse, she was picking it up from them.

She took to walking past the church at all hours, until Edelfish and the girls noticed she had gone off by herself and retrieved her. And so for two weeks while Edelfish scoured possibilities for investment, Mrs. Edelfish roamed the town and countryside with an eye for something else. Edelfish closed his eye to his wife's new interest. It was a phase she was going through, he was sure. Age and a woman's change of life were responsible, he was sure, and though the fat bounced solidly when she moved, he would make sure she ate better and didn't skip any of her three meals per day.

The beginning of the third week of their sojourn in town, the Edelfish girls had to force her away from a young soldier she was smothering with attention, and mollified her attempts to bring him home for the evening meal. Papa would be upset and his cousin, well, where could they put another at the table already overflowing with guests?

Lemish knew Edelfish slightly. Nodded to him in the morning when their paths crossed in the market or town. He had heard of Edelfish's dilemma and his business. One morning the sun was shining when Mrs. Edelfish decided to sneak off by herself for a shopping jaunt. All in the house were still asleep so she slipped off and went into town. The town was quiet so she continued walking toward the main road, the road by which the vendors' brought their produce to market. But it was quiet today. A holiday she wasn't aware of. She sauntered along the road, picked a few berries and finding a quiet grassy knoll by the edge of the road, sat. The sun warmed the earth and through her dress she felt the young morning warmth predicting a hot day. She fell asleep.

Meeme Ruchel walked from her house to town. She took the road, the same road the vendors took through the fields. Clumping her way along with her stick, scattering twigs and leaves in her path to see what treasures she would stir up that might be hiding. Bent almost to the ground, she saw only the few feet beneath her. Suddenly she almost stumbled coming upon a heap of printed cotton. Mrs. Edelfish spread out on the grassy knoll, a kerchief covering her face and eyes from the sun. Meeme Ruchel tapped her find.

"You there, you're in my way."

Mrs. Edelfish woke, startled, "Who? What—?" Then she saw Ruchel, the wart on her nose peeking through straggling hair.

"What do you want?" she asked Ruchel. "I'm just resting."

Meeme Ruchel tapped Mrs. Edelfish's leg with her stick. "What I find in my way, I take home with me," she said.

"I'm not in your way," said Mrs. Edelfish indignantly smoothing her skirt. "I'm on the side of the road. Look at all the room you have to walk around me," she pointed.

Meeme Ruchel shook her head and her stick.

"I don't walk around anything. Follow me." She took Mrs. Edelfish by the hand, gripping her cane like a cudgel in the other. Mrs. Edelfish went.

Meeme Ruchel marched Mrs. Edelfish home. Lemish had awakened and washed and was waiting to fix a bite to eat for breakfast, when the door opened and Mrs. Edelfish was marched in by his wife, who with her cane then proceeded to push her toward the bed and then under the bed into her hiding place. Down went Mrs. Edelfish under the pallet. She lay there curious but not uncomfortable. She curled up, pushing her buttocks toward the opening, and proceeded to pull up her skirts. Dressing, Lemish turned gray and tried to hide the sight from his wife. When Meeme Ruchel saw the bared buttocks gleaming from the floor, she took her cane and whacked them.

Lemish paled, "Stop Ruchel. You can't strike her."

"She belongs to me. I found her, didn't I?"

Mr. Edelfish was brought to the house by Lemish, the two daughters in tow giggling fearfully. Edelfish was shocked to find his wife in her position, nesting comfortably under the bed. He bent down to lift her up but she shook her head no and laid it down again on her criss-crossed arms, her buttocks still held high under her knees.

"Come Frendle," Mr. Edelfish urged, "it's time to go home. I will put you in your comfortable bed. Come home, dear."

The reclining form shook its head and closed its eyes. Mr. Edelfish nodded for the girls to help him and he began to tug at her. Meeme Ruchel flew at him with her stick.

"Hands off my things, you thief!" she screamed.

"Woman, are you mad, out of your mind? This is my wife!"

"I found her—she's mine now and besides," Meeme Ruchel whistled through her teeth, "she doesn't want to go with you. Ask her."

"Frendle, come home." Mr. Edelfish turned to the underpart of the pallet. "Don't be childish, come home with us," he urged.

The mound lay unmoved, unmoving, nestling, asleep. Lemish sat down to breakfast and the Edelfishes walked back to the schochat's house.

A Dybbuk in the Soup

FRIMME GENZEL of Pedeshva was waiting to hear from her sister in Yarmalinitz. She had written to Blume when Blume had sent word by the traveling schochet that her eldest son Mechel was restless again and she wanted Frimme to take him for a few weeks. He needed a change, Blume said. He or she—it didn't matter.

Frimme knew of the difficulties Blume's eldest perpetrated. Perpetrated or invited. It ended the same way. Lack of mozel or schlimozel dogged his footsteps. It was always off season for Jews when he applied to the university. Finally he was sent to Cracow. The boy was so brilliant, such a chuchim that when a lecturer made an error Mechel corrected him. After all a goyishe kopf—Mechel was correct but he was sent home. The university could do without Mechel. The fools, Blume said indignantly.

So Mechel came home. He had no patience to teach young children and bring in fifty zlotys a week—he needed something more challenging, intellectually stimulating. Twice a week he would argue with the Rabbi on some theological point until the Rebbetzin threw him out when she saw her husband gagging with rage.

Once Mechel had been told to stop thinking and work physically, so he wouldn't wear his mind out. So he took a pick and helped

Schloime Baruch with his farming. His finger blistered from the work and became infected. They soaked it in salt for two weeks. Schloime then asked him to help with his three cows, Lubka, Kalinka and Miske; but Mechel didn't like the way they looked at him. So Blume was sending Mechel to her—to find himself, to rest a little. That's what comes of having too bright a boy.

Frimme Genzel's own son was not so bright so he worked in the fields. He had good arms and strong shoulders and made even patches for vegetables. He could count three seeds for each hole he dug and cover them.

Her daughter, on the other hand, was too bright. She knew how to read and write and dreamed her day away, waiting for a Rabbi or a great man to find her. If she fed the chickens in the morning she was exhausted for the rest of the day, and she would stretch out in front of the hearth and watch the fire. Her eyes glazed on the fire; her dreams rose and fell with the leaping flames. By nightfall she was drained, extinguished, and would scarce answer Frimme's request for her to set the table for dinner.

What comes of having such gifted children? They are never appreciated.

Frimme stirred the soup. She added another pinch of salt and tasted it again. There was something lacking; the chicken soup was flat. The carrot was there, the onion, the greens in it—still it was lacking. She stirred it vigorously again and spooned some of the fat off the watery surface.

Such wonderful children. Such talent. So Blume said. What things they would accomplish when they came to themselves. When they put their feet on the solid track and walked in one direction. She tasted the soup. Removed the chicken from the pot onto a plate. Lifted the pot and threw the soup out the back door. She started grating beets for borscht.

Dunya's Dybbuk

THE MORNING WENT bleakly for Dunya. The handle of the broom broke as she was swinging it to unhinge a spider web from one stubborn corner of the small cottage she shared with her old mother. She began to knead the dough on the board for the challah while she waited for her mother to return from Shimme the schochat's with the chicken they would cook for the Sabbath meal that evening.

She flattened the dough with her fingers and then took the long wooden rolling pin to it. She rolled it lengthwise. The dough flattened into an oblong. She crisscrossed the rolling pin to widen it. The dough began to fray and split along the edges. Dunya balled the dough up, again flattened it, and began to roll over it with the rolling pin. This time the planed dough split smack center. Again Dunya kneaded it into a ball, and added a bit of water. Rolled it out. Too watery. She could not lift the dough from the board. It adhered in large chunks. An egg added; another pinch of salt. She kneaded. Flattened. Rolled. The dough fell into strips. Flaked. Lumped. She could not roll it into the traditional three strips to braid the challah. At other times she would have laughed at her angry frustration with the resistant dough. A dybbuk she muttered to the balled dough.

Hastily throwing a cloth over the dough, in tears she grabbed an armful of soiled clothes and stamped out of the hut to go to the brook. Mama would understand when she saw the raw dough and would finish the job. Perhaps she would have better luck.

Dunya walked out toward the rocks that lay along the creek. She rolled her skirt under her waist and walked onto the rocks to lay the clothes out. She dipped a blouse into the cold water and began to thrash it against the round worn wash rocks. She kneaded the blouse, wrung it out and held it up to the light that fitered through the trees flanking the cool swift running brook. The stains and soil would not leave the fabric. She immersed the blouse in water again and rubbed the stains between her fingers. They would not budge. She took a petticoat and began to wash it. Immersing. Thrashing. Scrubbing. The gray soil would not leave the cloth. The sun now beat down. She folded her arms over her knees and leaned her head on her arms.

Nothing was right today. A dybbuk was pursuing her. She would ask Reb Nahum tomorrow after the Sabbath. She sat for a long while and then, realizing the hour, stood to gather up the clothes.

Her arms full of clothes she heard the bush behind her break suddenly. There on horse, saber raised, a red-eyed drunken Cossack. The saber swung at her as she turned to run. She stumbled to her knees on the rocks and with surprise watched her blood seep over the clothes into the brook.

The Doctor

THE DOCTOR CHECKED his instruments in the little case near the window. The morning sun was full in the window and dancing particles spun quietly through the light beams. The children were still sleeping upstairs and Polya was bustling the servants through the breakfast chores. A peasant had alerted him earlier that an accident was being brought to him—a minor wound—perhaps a broken bone, nothing that would take him out. Moynka, one of the peasants at the mill, had injured his hand or foot. He would know momentarily. His equipment was ready; a boiling pot of water containing his instruments was already simmering on the large iron stove in the kitchen.

"Alexei, they are here," Polya announced to him through the open door.

"Pan Oblensky, we have to trouble you so early and on Sunday, too." Volka, the night watchman at the mill, swept into the room, his dilapidated fur cap in his hand. "This ass leaned too close to the blade last night." The doctor looked at the man standing next to Volka. The man hugged his rag-wrapped right arm close to his body, and supported its weight with his other arm.

"Last night, and you waited until now?"

"We didn't think it was so serious. We've all had cuts at the mill—if you saw every little scratch...."

"Here, sit him down." The doctor pointed to a chair. The man's face was blanched around his black beard tinged with sawdust, his eyes blackly sunken. He extended the wrapped arm. As Doctor Oblensky slowly unwrapped the arm, the fresh blood welled through the white sheet strips binding the wound. Red drops splattered on the floor. The doctor exposed the gash, opened to the bone. He wrapped a clean towel around it.

"Volka, move the screen and lay him on the examining table." He nodded toward the corner of the room. Volka helped Moynka to his feet and led him stumbling to the cot.

"His wife made such a noise at the mill master's door that he sent me to look at him. She wouldn't quiet down until I promised to send for you, but since he could walk...my time is worth less than six groshen, so I hitched up the horses...."

The doctor took the ether bottle out of a cabinet and turned to Volka. "Go into the kitchen and help the maid bring the boiling pot in here. She'll show you how to empty the water to lighten it. Whatever you do, don't touch the inside of the pot. Watch the maid. Pani Oblensky will direct you. He has lost a great deal of blood." The doctor put the ether-soaked rag on the man's face.

"Breathe deeply. Don't be afraid. I only want to fix your arm. Yes, breath so—that's good." Volka came in with the steaming pot.

"Put it on that table. Fine." The doctor took a pair of forceps from the instrument case and began removing the scalpel, scissors, and suture needles from the pot. He laid them on a clean towel on the table next to the cot.

The clang of the church bells came through the open window. Soon the peasants would be congregating for mass. He and Polya would be there too especially on this day, Easter Sunday. Volka leaned over Moynka's legs, watching the doctor.

"It's too bad," said Volka. "Poor Moynka will miss all the fun."

"What fun?" asked the doctor.

"Killing the Jews."

"What?"

"Killing the Jews in the village. The Czar said in his speech yesterday that the new Russia had no use for such vermin—the Christ killers."

Doctor Oblensky looked at the open smiling face near his. He cleaned the wound with soap and water. Christ killers. He had heard how these good Christians butchered Jews. Murdered men, women, children; not even babes were spared in this fury—this fury of righteousness. He shuddered within himself.

"Poor Moynka," said Volka. "Maybe we can save a Jew or two for him. Not a pogrom for him since the one in Galizia a few years ago. He was a regular Cossack then. He would catch two at a time in his arms and crack their skulls." Volka smiled beneficently down at the sleeping Moynka.The doctor began to stitch the wound. "And besides," Volka continued, "he had his eye on Moshe Baer's daughter—the older pretty one." The doctor looked up at Volka. Volka smiled and winked. "A man's entitled to a little fun when he's doing God's work for the Czar."

Moshe Baer the shoemaker had two lovely daughters. He had seen Bettya, the older one, recently for a chest cold. A gay laughing girl with large blue eyes and fair skin. . . . She wore her blonde hair loose to the hips. Her mother had to coax her into disrobing for the examination. What would the respectful, smiling face watching him show if he knew that Dr. Oblensky came from these people? It had been a long time since he thought of that.

As a boy, Nissun Ben Cohen had wanted to go to the University of Berlin, and his father, a well-off wine merchant, had permitted it against his mother's wishes. And then, after he returned two years later and told them that he had chosen medicine which was closed to Jews, his mother cried and blamed his father for sending him to study among Christians. His father, when he realized that Nissun was adamant and would no longer listen to any reasoning, tore his lapels and entered into a period of mourning befitting the death of a son of Israel. His father sat shiva the whole week. He, in the meantime, went to a priest, who in turn sent him on to another priest in a larger city for instruction. He became Alexei Oblensky and rejoined his group of students at the University, fellow students who, like himself, read the great philosophers and believed in the brotherhood of all men.

Since that time many years ago he had heard that there had been two pogroms in Vilna. Often he had thought of his younger sister, Brontsya. Sweet Brontsya with her soft curls and saucy dancing eyes. Such thoughts were no good for him. Long ago he had chosen life. The life that the universality of his soul called for. The life which owes its existence to no traditional God—but which transcends God as a life-giving force and seeks this Godliness in all men, and sees in each man the sameness of being, as to each man is allowed the same sky. He looked out of the open window into the soft spring sky with an occasional flitting bird winging across the horizon. The fruit trees were covered with delicately colored blossoms. He closed the wound and wrapped a fresh gauze around the arm.

"Let him rest awhile," he said to Volka as he finished. "Sit here with him."

He walked out of the room and into the kitchen. Polya looked up from her cup of tea as he came in.

"Alexei, some tea? The samovar has just been heated."

He nodded and sat down on a chair across the table from her. She got up to get a fresh cup. It was one of the newly imported ones from England.

"We are fancy today," he said.

"It's Easter, and besides, I wanted an excuse to use them."

Alexei smiled up at her as she poured his tea. A hairpin was hanging precariously from the bun at the nape of her neck. In a minute she would catch it and secure it firmly in the bun. She was still a handsome woman. Heavier, but still as gay and witty as the somewhat gauche but militantly liberal student she was when he met her at the University. He had been seeing a great deal of Ivana, that beautiful journalism student from Moscow, when he met Polya. Her family had objected to him at first—a converted

Jew. But when her grand-aunt the Duchess of Rostofska met him and approved the match, the family followed suit and they were married by the Bishop of Strega. Alexei had his first communion and then the second. He found the religious studies not difficult, and applied himself as diligently to those as he tried diligently to forget his earlier learning. They reached the height of respectability when the Grand Duchess of Svetlova herself invited the young couple to tea.

Alexei thought of Moshe Baer's family. How could he get word to them?

"You're very deep in thought, darling," said Polya.

"Did you know that a pogrom is planned today?"

"Manya chattered about something, but I hardly pay attention to her. Why are you so concerned? This doesn't affect you."

"That's true. I am no longer a Jew. I haven't been one for almost thirty years. Why is this happening now?"

"Now?"

"I must go warn them."

"You can't. You're crazy."

"Why not? Maybe they can run and save themselves. At least let them not be taken unaware and slaughtered."

She thrust herself into the doorway in front of him.

"You must not do this. You will destroy us....The children...."

He stared at her. "Is this the liberal student I married? The one who once protested so vehemently the rights of all men?"

"But they're only Jews."

"And a Jew is not a man?"

"It is for the good of Russia to destroy them."

"You really believe that?"

"Yes...yes!"

"And I, who was a Jew—am I better than they? Or worse?"

Alexei pushed past her through the doorway. He dashed across the narrow bridge which separated the newer section of town from the old. The Jews lived in small cottages huddled about their dilapidated little synagogue. Moshe Baer's shoe repair shop was in front of the house. The doctor ran to the back door and knocked. Sarah, Moshe Baer's wife, answered the door. She was visibly shocked to see the doctor but curtsied pleasantly.

"Is Moshe here?" The doctor glanced inside.

"I am here." Moshe walked in from the back room. "Dr. Oblensky!"

"Moshe, a pogrom is in the making!" Sarah gasped and ran into the girls' room.

"How do you know this?"

"I heard the peasants talking."

Moshe looked carefully at the doctor. "It is very kind of you to warn us, but go, you are in jeopardy if you are caught with us."

"You have no time to spare—run!" the doctor cried.

"We must tell the others. Sarah, run to the Benskys. Bettya to the Feinmans. The Rabbi must be warned. The men in the synagogue. Shaya, the woodcutter, his old father and the children. The Salinkys. Run, children!"

"Mass is almost over—go, Moshe!" said the doctor. From a distance they heard footsteps running toward them. Moshe turned from the doctor, ran into the kitchen and came back with two knives. The door burst open. Paul, the woodcutter's son stood in the doorway, his eyes gaping and his mouth panting. His ax dangling in one hand.

"Where are the girls?" Paul yelled hoarsely.

"We sent them to warn the others," said Sarah.

Rifka came running in. "Bettya is here, too," she panted breathlessly.

Paul crumbled to the floor and began to weep.

"They caught my father and grandfather near the church. . . . They caught them as they were driving the cart from the woods. Fifty of them with knives and clubs. . . ." he cried. Paul sobbed, "and I ran. . . I ran here. I couldn't help him! I couldn't help him! When he needed me, I ran. For God's sake, go, all of you!"

Bettya kneeled near Paul and gave him her hand. He stumbled to his feet. There were loud crashes and screams from the woods. The church bells rang loudly.

"We are surrounded!" yelled Paul.

"Go, doctor," Moshe felt the edge of the knives. "Bettyali, Rifkali, come here, children."

Sarah clenched her teeth to keep her sorrow within. The tears ran from her eyes. She kissed the girls and moved them toward their father. They knelt in front of him. The knife trembled in his hand. Rifka's hands trembled, her mouth quivered and whimpered. Bettya lifted her face toward her father. He brought the knife toward the girl's throat. Dr. Oblensky moved toward Moshe. Moshe, aware of his gesture, looked up and motioned him to stop with his hand.

"Sarah! Bring me my tallis," he called.

Sarah ran into the bedroom. Moshe turned to the doctor.

"It is a kindness I perform. May God accept it from me as he would have Isaac from Abraham."

Sarah brought in the tallis and wrapped it around Moshe's shoulders. She put the siddur in front of him.

"How can you?" cried the doctor.

"I saw what such a mob did to one of my friend's sisters—before they took out her eyes." His hands shook, "Please don't try to dissuade me. It is hard enough."

Moshe brushed the tears from his eyes. He smiled at the shivering girls in front of him. Paul stationed himself at the door. Sarah cried through her clenched teeth. Bettya put her hands on her father's knees.

"It's all right, Papa, it's all right." Her lips trembled in a smile.

He cupped her chin in one of his hands and leaned to kiss her face. He moved the knife quickly across her throat. The blood gushed from her neck as he lay her head on the floor. Rifka ran to the door. Paul held her from running out.

"Don't be afraid, child," Moshe cried.

She whimpered and sat near him. He covered her eyes and kissed her. Dr. Oblensky sat down near Bettya. He folded her body and closed her glazing eyes. He smoothed the blood-matted blonde hair. His hands trembled. Moshe lay Rifka near her sister. And then stood over his two daughters and stared. Sarah lay crumpled on the floor. Alexei realized that tears were dripping from his own face. Shouts came from the outside.

"Doctor, this is not a day for you to be found with Jews." Moshe pointed to the back door. "There may be a chance that way."

"I was born a Jew," the doctor said.

Moshe raised his eyebrows. "You have chosen a strange time to admit this. You have no reason to die with us."

"I wanted to go to the synagogue."

"It is probably already in flames."

Paul looked out of the window and sat himself near Bettya. He took one of her hands in his. The ax lay across his knees. The tears had dried on his cheeks.

Shouts suddenly surrounded the house. Paul leaped to his feet. The door latch broke under the weight straining against it. The door crashed open and peasants swarmed in. They threw themselves on Moshe. Paul hacked at them with the ax but was clubbed and quickly dismembered by a scythe. The women swept through the house and carried feather pillows out. Sarah never got up from the ground; her blood gushed from many wounds in her body.

Volka came in with another little band of peasants. Blood-spattered and red-eyed with drink, he looked puzzled when he noticed the doctor. Then he saw the bodies of the two girls.

"What dog did us out of our fun?" He wiped his mouth with the back of a blood-stained arm. The doctor stared at Volka's blood-spattered face and his wild eyes. One of the men following him took Volka's shoulders.

"Come on, we're finished here. Coblentz took the peddler's house."

An old woman came in.

"Holy Mother Russia is now cleansed," she said, crossing herself as she viewed the bodies in the room.

"Let's go!" Several grouped themselves near Volka and the doctor. They suddenly became aware of the physician's presence. But one didn't question Dr. Oblensky. The men shuffled their feet waiting for Volka.

"You were to stay with Moynka," the doctor said to Volka.

"He didn't need me after your excellent care. Would it be impertinent for me to inquire what the doctor is doing in the house of a Jew?"

"A doctor treats all human beings."

"I didn't know anyone here was sick; besides I don't think they can use your services any more."

Volka laughed and pulled a bottle out of his coat pocket.

"Too bad you can't put them together like Moynka's arm."

The others laughed. Volka walked toward the bodies of the two girls and lifted up Bettya's dress and put his hand underneath.

"Stop that! For God's sake, leave her alone!" Alexei yelled.

"You liked her too, eh? What a one to warm a bed with, those flashing eyes."

The crowd near the door was suddenly thrust apart by the village priest with Polya hanging close behind.

"Father, save him! Save him!" she cried before she saw Alexei.

"Alexei Oblensky, are you an apostate?" The priest hurled the words at Alexei in deliberate ponderous tones.

"No, I am not," answered the doctor.

"Of course, he is not, father. He is a good Christian. He was certified by the Bishop of Strega," interceded Polya.

The priest shrugged her off. He addressed himself to Alexei again.

"Alexei Oblensky, is it true you were born Nissun Ben Cohen?" Volka and the others crowded closer around them.

"Yes," answered the doctor.

"You promised not to tell, only to save him if there was trouble," Polya cried.

"Daughter, he was found in dangerous circumstances and must prove himself."

"So the renowned doctor is a Jew," Volka grimaced mockingly.

"No, he is a good Christan. . . . You all know that." Polya looked around askingly.

The peasants began to shuffle toward him.

"Wait my children. We will interrogate him," said the priest.

"If he's a Jew, that's all we have to know," one of the peasants near the door shouted.

The crowd surged into the room again.

"This for a Russian woman who has to do with Jews!" A woman slapped Polya and spit in her face. The men tore her clothes off and tossed her to and from each other. The priest murmured prayers for her. Nissun never saw the blow. He lay where he fell.

And Next Year

THE SUNLIT VILLAGE was set in the midst of the wheat fields. The short irregular little streets of the spring-warmed Ukrainian village became narrow paths as they led through the fields and into the open grassy meadow at the back of the town. The old part of the town was on the slight incline of a small hill; the newer section nestled close to it, separated by a narrow brook and bridged by wooden planks reinforced with stone and mortar.

Usually, at this time of day, people and animals walked in the noon sunlight. They moved in and out of town and the narrow streets were clogged with people going about their business, chasing goats and fowls to clear a path for themselves. Today it was quiet in the sunlight. The flies buzzed as usual and a lone chicken flapped its way from a window sill to the ground and clucked and strutted about imperiously.

The synagogue stood in the old town; a tiny wooden building with a large crooked stone for a threshold and badly hinged doors. It was old and covered with signs of futile repair. Inside the old Rabbi tottered between the chairs and adjusted the curtains of the ark in the center of the one-room synagogue. He pulled his tallis closer to him and adjusted it as it dropped off his shoulder. He delicately moved the curtains apart, exposing the ark doors behind them. Lovingly he examined the cloth between his fingers as he pushed the curtains aside. Behind the doors was housed the Torah—the sacred scrolls he had studied for years and prayed from.

He walked down from the bema and sat down in one of the seats facing the ark in the dusty stillness of the synagogue—the rays of the sun came in slowly through the small narrow windows under the roof. The stillness creaked as the weary Rabbi beheld the ark.

Yesterday at this time Fanya Gittel had burst in on him, while he was with a student, with a loud grievous complaint about Motyah Fetter Sheeyah's cow. The cow had wandered away from the field and in walking past her house had knocked over two pails of fresh milk. Motyah refused to make good for his cow's damage, and he, the Rabbi, had to make peace and render justice on behalf of the plaintiff.

The Rabbi calmed Fanya a little and Motyah who waited outside the synagogue with the guilty cow. Motyah refused to take responsibility for the act of a dumb unthinking animal—the buckets should not have been standing unguarded in front of Fanya Gittel's doorstep. What if a child had knocked them over? After much talking with both, Motyah agreed to replace the milk in the buckets, since Fanya's young children depended on this sustenance; and Motyah Feter Sheeyah was a good, generous, amiable man in the Rabbi's eyes, and it was fitting for him to be benevolent to the widow Fanya Gittel.

This was yesterday; the same sun shone outdoors in the spring air. He had sent Fanya and her children to the woods. He hoped none of the Jews remained in the village or took to the cellars, which he had warned against their doing. He remembered hearing how they had burned the Jews in the cellars in which they were hiding in Proskorov a few years ago. They had opened the doors and thrown in dried wood and fire brands. He shut his eyes and bent his head. He had served this town as Rabbi for sixty years. His father had been a Rabbi in this very synagogue when he was a boy. He was a young man away at the Yeshiva when the pogrom had broken out. His father had sent his wife and younger children away with the other Jewish villagers. Some of them had been hidden by gentile neighbors, some found refuge in the gypsy camp nearby. Drunken peasants and Cossacks swooped down from the hills. In their fright the people had forgotten to remove the Torah from the ark. His father had urged them to run and had taken the Torah from the ark.

With his hands and a little spade his father had dug a hole behind the synagogue. He wrapped the Torah in his tallis and laid it in the ground. He was covering it with soil when the horsemen came upon him. What treasure was the Jewish Rabbi burying? They didn't ask. Two jumped off their horses and began digging in the soft dirt. They pulled up the tallis-wrapped scrolls out of the ground, ripped off the tallis and with their swords cut the velvet off the scrolls. They unrolled the parchment and tore it apart. In anger one ran his sword through the Rabbi and left him twitching on the ground until he died.

The old Rabbi raised his eyes to the ark. "Oh my God," he said to himself, "why have you given us so much faith and knowledge and no understanding of why these things should be? For what are we being punished? For our belief in you? For our love of you? Since the destruction of the second temple, such a history—Masada, York, Spain." Since the beginning of the Mendel Beilis trial he knew Russia was brooding. The trumped-up blood ritual murder—the old charge to pierce Jews with. Each Easter they quaked when the peasants drank too much. "And next year in Jerusalem," they had just finished praying in the Passover seder, please God, or the next or the next—for almost two thousand years this had been the prayer. And when? Dear God, when?

The tears rolled down the Rabbis' face and into his long, old, white beard. When can we live in peace? Pray in peace? See children grow without fear, without the hiding and running and the dying. In his youth he had run. What was there to run from now? Death? He had already died twice before, once when he and

Sarah had buried their tiny firstborn son, and again when Sarah died. He had taken his father's death bitterly, but the sorrow was comforted with the anger of youth. His comfort now was the Torah—its words, its wisdom and teachings. Selfishly, perhaps, he had refused to let the other Jews take it to the woods to bury. Perhaps the trouble would fly over, he had told them. Let us hope—leave it with him, he had asked. They agreed—there was no time for debate—and they ran to the woods beyond the fields and some took goat carts in the hope of reaching the larger cities to the north of them.

He heard the church bell from the other end of town. The Rabbi got up slowly and opened the ark—he bound his tefillin around his arm, "Shma Yisroel"—deliver us from evil though I walk through the valley of death. He heard voices below the hillock. Suddenly he had an urge to urinate. He went to the door quickly. . . . He would not defile the house of the lord in his fright. Urine and blood—the essence of man's being. He went toward the door and knew the knives were flashing in the sunlight.